Matt Crim

Adventures of a Fair Rebel

Matt Crim

Adventures of a Fair Rebel

ISBN/EAN: 9783337339968

Printed in Europe, USA, Canada, Australia, Japan

Cover: Foto ©Andreas Hilbeck / pixelio.de

More available books at **www.hansebooks.com**

ADVENTURES OF

A FAIR REBEL.

BY

MATT CRIM.

New York :

CHARLES L. WEBSTER & CO.

1891.

PRESS OF
JENKINS & McCowan,
NEW YORK.

ADVENTURES OF A FAIR REBEL.

CHAPTER I.

IT was in the second year of the war that my uncle, Charles Dillingham, decided to sell his plantation in western North Carolina, and, with his family and slaves, return to the old homestead near Decatur, Georgia, a small town a few miles below Atlanta.

There were only three of the Dillingham heirs—my mother, Uncle Charles and Uncle Reuben. On my mother's marriage her portion of the property had been given to her, but the two brothers lived together, even after Uncle Charles married a North Carolina girl. My cousins, Alicia and Nell, were ten and five years of age respectively when their mother grew homesick for the wilds of her native State, and pleaded to return. My parents were both dead, so I lived with my uncles. The brothers divided their property, Uncle Charles taking his portion in money and slaves, and we journeyed to the old North State to live.

In a few years my aunt died, and we children longed to go back to the old home in Georgia, but it seemed hard for Uncle Charles to move again. Every year he put it off, until the war came on, and Uncle Reuben died, wifeless and childless, leaving the homestead and family slaves to his brother. Even then Uncle Charles hesitated about returning, for he had a vein of weakness in his fine character which prevented him from ever being positive about anything—even his business affairs.

After much thought and talk, and many arguments from us, he decided to go. We palpitated with delight, and could talk of nothing else. The negroes were also wild with joy—for, in the division, many had been separated from those near and dear to them. In the " big house " and in the cabins a note of preparation was sounded.

I had only two servants—an old man and his wife. Uncle Ned had been my father's devoted slave and body-servant, and Aunt Milly my nurse and maid. They were my attendants—my body-guard. They watched over me with sleepless vigilance, served me with tenderest love. Aunt Milly was a tall, strong woman, with gentle manners and a rather uncertain temper; Uncle Ned, lean, erect and dignified. His black face had shriveled into a network of wrinkles; his hair looked like white wool. He had a great deal of family pride, and, I think, secretly regarded himself as my true guardian. What irrepressible joy those two old people betrayed when they learned that we were really going back!

" Lawd, honey, has Mars Charles made up his mind, sho' 'nough ? " cried Uncle Ned, when I ran into the room where he was at work cleaning and polishing my shoes, while Aunt Milly sewed on my new gown.

" He has," I cried, capering about the room in my excessive delight.

Tears ran down Aunt Milly's face, and she rocked to and fro with many ejaculations and pious words.   Uncle Ned took it more quietly.

"Dar ain't no country like Georgey," he said, emphatically.

Uncle Charles wished to send my cousins and me under a suitable escort around by rail, while he traveled across the country and through the mountains with the slaves; but we were so anxious to go with him that he yielded to our importunities.

Alicia entertained a good many fears of the journey, and indulged in dark forebodings. She was a tall, very slender girl, of twenty-four, one year older than I. She had long arms, a long, delicate neck, and a long nose. Her chin retreated slightly, and her complexion was pale. She possessed no beauty, except her fine brown hair and dark, soft, short-sighted eyes.   Her height and the deficiency in her vision caused her to lean forward, until she stooped habitually.   She was a refined and delicate creature, with a great deal of timidity

in her nature, and a world of sentiment hidden
under sedate manners. She had strength of
character in some ways, for Uncle Charles leaned on her judgment, and I often thought that
he loved her more tenderly than he did Nell.
She was so gentle, sympathized with him so
understandingly, and had such patience with
his vacillating weakness.

Nell was eighteen, and one of the prettiest
girls in the country. She was a coquette, devoting a good deal of time to her curls and her
dress. She was spoiled, had scornful ways,
and people admired but did not always love
her.

The first thing that I did toward preparing
for the journey was to beg my uncle for a pistol—for who could tell what adventures might,
or might not, befall us? I enjoyed the prospect of being waylaid by highwaymen, for I
had read Byron and Scott until my head was
full of romance. Southern girls before the war
were bred and brought up in an atmosphere of
chivalry and knight-errantry. My uncle laugh-

ed at me, but I persisted in my entreaty for a weapon.

"You would only shoot yourself," he said, at last.

"Try me, and see!" I cried, nettled at his lack of faith in my courage and good sense.

"You would never dare to shoot at any one, Rachel."

"If molested, I would. We may go into great dangers on this journey, and it is well to be prepared."

He gave me my way in the matter.

I can look back on that time and pity Uncle Charles. With three young women to guide and protect, his life must have been full of harassing experiences.

That summer seemed very long to us, though Uncle Charles grumbled at the shortness of time. Some of the crops were gathered; some were sold in the field. Household furniture had to be disposed of, and the things specially prized collected together and packed. At the last moment my uncle decided that the slaves bought in North Carolina must be sold there. He did not care to again separate families.

It was on a clear, frosty September morning that we started. Some of the negroes wept loudly at the breaking asunder of new ties, and we were near to tears as we parted from friends and neighbors. Our white-covered wagons, stored with tents, household treasures and provisions, stretched out like a caravan along the road. Nell and I were on horseback, Alicia and her father in the carriage. There were fifty negroes—men, women and children —and all those who could, walked. The young children and the feeble old people rode in the wagons.

In the excitement of travel we soon lost that first, keenest pang of regret for our friends. Nell remained pensive for a few hours, thinking of her lovers, but I rallied her so cruelly that she regained her usual spirits. I had left no binding heart-interests to tear cords of love asunder. Love I had not experienced, though

three-and-twenty and full of ardent sentiment
and feeling.   I was not so handsome as my
cousin Nell, nor so plain as Alicia.   My features were irregular, my skin clear and smooth.
I had brilliant dark blue eyes and black hair.
I was regarded as an accomplished girl, and
one above the average in intellect.   I could
play on the piano, possessed a good contralto
voice, and had made myself familiar with all
the readable books in my uncle's library.   I
had received two offers of marriage, but, beyond flattering my vanity, they had made no
impression on me.

That first day's travel passed without incident, and we camped on the bank of a creek
under the shadow of the mountains.   Our tents
were pitched, and pine boughs were laid thickly on the ground for the beds to rest upon.   We
had supper between sunset and dark, and then
the negroes cooked their rations for the next
day.   As the frosty night came on they gathered closely about the camp-fires and sang
corn-field melodies, the mellow notes coming

back from the mountain-passes in a thousand sweet echoes.

We slept that night with the pungent odors of hemlock and spruce about us, and the sound of falling water in our ears.

The next day we journeyed through the mountains, the scenery growing wilder and wilder as we penetrated the defiles or toiled over the foothills. My horse went lame about midday in one of its forefeet, and several of the negroes examined it without being able to find the cause; then Uncle Ned carefully and gravely looked at the hoof.

"H'm! Miss Rachel, honey, it looks mighty like it's been conjured. If it was a stone, it stands to reason we might see it."

"Chut!" cried Uncle Charles, contemptuously; "let me see what is the matter."

But he discovered no more than the negroes, and I had to ride in the carriage, while the poor horse was tied to the back of one of the wagons, and limped along, apparently in much pain.

2

The negroes looked on the animal with awe, certain that it had been conjured; and though Uncle Charles scolded them sharply, they were not shaken in their superstitious belief. It cast a slight gloom over them, and other misfortunes were expected.

As the day declined the weather changed. The wind blew from the south, and clouds gathered threateningly. We went into camp early, and deep trenches were dug out around our tents. The prospect of a storm depressed my uncle, and made the negroes anxious. It was the wildest night any of us had ever been abroad. Rain fell in torrents, and the wind shrieked through the mountains like a hurricane. Alicia, Nell and I occupied one tent. We huddled down under the blankets and listened to the roar of the tempest, pitying the poor horses for having no shelter except the dripping trees. Uncle Charles came to the tent door.

"Girls, girls, are you comfortable?" he cried, anxiously.

We assured him that we were, and enjoying the situation.

Alicia and Nell finally slept, but excitement kept me awake. I rose, and, groping my way to the tent door, unfastened a corner of the canvas. A cold spray beat in my face; the wind nearly took my breath away. Two of the wagons were within range of my vision, and under one of them a lighted lantern had been hung. It swayed to and fro, casting a pale glimmer on the ground. Beyond its feeble glow the world was blotted out in a darkness so intense that no human eye could penetrate it. Uncle Charles passed by the tent with another lantern. He was wrapped in an oil-cloth coat reaching to the top of his high, coarse boots. I softly called to him. He stopped, bending slightly before the gale.

"Any danger?" I inquired.

"Not unless the tents are blown away."

I listened, dismayed, and the situation assumed a more serious aspect. It was one thing to be housed, dry and warm, under thick canvas—another to be exposed to the pitiless fury of the storm.

" Do you think they *will* be blown away ? "

" I cannot tell," he said, grimly. " I was a fool to allow you girls to take the hardships of this trip. Go back to bed, and sleep. It will be time enough for alarm when the tent-poles give way."

" Why don't you lie down, Uncle Charles ? "

" I intend to, as soon as I look after the horses."

Though wind and rain roared like a great sea lashed to fury, and the earth seemed to tremble sometimes beneath us, the tents withstood the tempest.

I fell asleep, but toward morning was wakened by Nell.

" Mother of mercy ! what is the matter ? " I exclaimed, startled by the vigorous shaking she gave me.

" There is a leak in the tent, Rachel. It is dripping in my face ! "

My own hair was moist, and when I threw

out my hand on the coverlid I found little
pools of water collecting in the quilted hollows. The long and violent rain had soaked
the thick canvas until large drops were falling
on us from the inner side. From that time
until daylight we were kept busy dodging the
leaks.

It was a gray morning, with lowering clouds
above and a wet earth below. The charred
remnants of the camp-fires were floating about
in ponds of water, and it was useless to try to
kindle new ones. After a cold, hasty breakfast
the teams were harnessed to the wagons, and
we set out on a dreary day's travel. The country through which we passed was very sparsely
settled. A cabin, set in the midst of a clearing,
here and there, seemed the only habitation of
man. The roads were rough, and the streams
we had to cross were so swollen by the rains
that it was dangerous to ford them. We met
two or three mountaineers, but they were sus-
picious and shy, and would have little to say
to us.

My poor Lightfoot continued to limp, and by midday one of the draught horses was reported lame. The negroes grew more and more uneasy, and two or three malcontents openly expressed dissatisfaction. Uncle Charles could exercise great firmness when it came to the control of his slaves. He rode all day in the rain, alternately cheering and lecturing the discontented ones.

"Brace up, boys, brace up! Remember that we are going home. What is a little rain? I don't mind it."

I could see, now, that it would have been much better for us to have gone the way he wished. We added greatly to his responsibility and care. Alicia, who was a fragile creature, suffered from the dampness, and the cold, unpalatable food, but Nell and I were both so strong and healthy that we could eat dry cornbread—"corn-pone"—and find it good. We passed the day singing and telling stories, and watched from the carriage windows for scenes of life along the road. We could not tell how high the mountains were above us, for their summits were lost in clouds and mist. Occasionally we caught glimpses of muddy waterfalls leaping and roaring down steep hillsides into the ravines below. Before the day closed, even I had lost all desire for excitement and adventure. A shelter, however rude; a fireside, however humble, would have satisfied me.

CHAPTER II.

THE short afternoon closed in very quickly. First the distant ranges faded from our vision, then out of the ravines and hollows black night seemed to spring upon us. The rain still fell steadily, and to go into camp with tents and bedclothes all wet, and no hope of having a fire, seemed utterly impossible. We pushed on until we finally came upon one of the lonely farm-houses, and my uncle decided to ask shelter for us. The rude cabin, with its small outhouses, stood on one side of the road, and a blacksmith's shop on the other. Two men were at work in it, and the ring of hammer and anvil, the red glow of firelight filling the sooty interior, thrilled us with a sense of companion-ship and warmth. An old man came to the door of the shop to parley with Uncle Charles, and in spite of the deep clamorous barking of dogs in the farm-yard, and the chatter of a

swarm of children peering at us from the doorstep, I overheard part of the conversation.

The old man stared out deliberately at the
wagons when my uncle requested a night's
lodging.

"'Pears to me there's a good many of you."

"Take in the three ladies. I can sleep any-
where, and the negroes will remain in the
wagons."

"All them niggers yourn?"

"Yes," impatiently.

"Secesh, air you?"

"Of course."

"Well, I ain't, but I don't know as that
would hinder us from takin' you in. Where
did you say you was from?"

"North Carolina."

"An' you are goin' down near Atlanty?"

"Yes."

"Had a brother livin' down somewhere in
them diggin's, but when they fust tuk to conscriptin' soldiers, he come back to the mountains."

" Can we stay ? " Uncle Charles inquired.

" I'll go an' ax the old woman."

He went across the road to the house. " I will pay handsomely for the lodging, and our servants can cook supper for us," Uncle Charles said eagerly, following him.

" Lord, man, we ain't a-hankerin' for money, though I don't say it ain't a good thing to have sometimes. If the wimmen fo'ks can stay they'll be welcome."

At last we were invited to alight and go in. Aunt Milly pressed up to the carriage as I stepped out, her face expressive of affection and sympathy.

" How *is* you feelin', honey ? "

" Cramped and stiff, but otherwise all right," I said cheerfully. " How are you ? "

" Lawd, chile, dem rheumaticks is got me dis time, sho. My ole j'ints feels lack dey gwine to brake to pieces."

" Is you gwine to keep Miss Rachel standin' in de rain all night, Milly, while you talk about your j'ints ? " Uncle Ned exclaimed, pushing her aside to hold an umbrella over me.

She seized an armful of wraps, and followed us to the house, and would not leave me until she inspected the bed we were to sleep on that night.

" It's better'n nuffin', dat's all I kin say," she whispered with a sniff of contempt.

The house had originally been one large room, but the back was finally cut off by a rude partition; then one run through it, making two small rooms. We learned that there were eighteen in family, fifteen children of all sizes and ages, the old man and his wife, and an aged grandmother.

A huge fireplace. half filled one end of the main room, and we gathered about it, the warmth and light of the burning logs on the hearth very grateful to us. The room was scantily furnished. Two beds, a dining-table and some chairs were the principal articles. In a corner of the hearth were piled the cooking utensils, and over the mantel hung strings of red pepper, seed okra still in the pod, and a bundle of gourds. The toothless, shriveled old grandmother sat in the chimney corner smoking a cob pipe. She entered into conversation with Alicia, and two rosy, dark-eyed young women drew near to listen. Nell was contented to nestle down by the fire and bask in its warmth, but I went to the door again to see what was going on outside.

The wagons had been drawn to the roadside, and the tired horses, released from the shafts, were munching their corn and fodder under a shelter at the end of the blacksmith's shop. The negroes had crowded into the shop, and were cooking by the furnace fire, a thick fog of steam rising from their moist clothes. House-servants and field-hands were joining amiably in getting up the repast, and I was glad to see them cheerful once more. Espying me in the doorway, vigilant Uncle Ned came over to see if I wanted anything.

A happy thought struck me.

"Yes, I want one of those blacksmiths to

examine Lightfoot's hoof. Perhaps there is something wrong with his shoe."

He eyed me reproachfully.

"Now, Miss Rachel, honey, what's de use o' dat? Didn't we all look at dat creetur's foot, even to Mars Chawles? you ain't gwine to find de cause o' dat limpin'; sho' es I live."

"You must do as I say, Uncle Ned," I replied, firmly.

"To be shore, honey. I al'ays do dat."

"So you're a Secesh, air you?" our host said to Uncle Charles, when they sat down by the fire after supper.

"I am, as I think every man ought to be at this time."

"Well, I don't know about that. To me the Union is o' more importance than all the niggers in creation."

"We are not fighting for the negroes, but State rights."

"'Mounts to the same thing, when it's sifted down. Me an' my boys keep out'n the fray. We can't fight for the Union, and we ain't goin' to fight agin it. Some in this part o' the country do fight for it in a sly way; that is, they're apt to make trouble for the rebs who come along."

My uncle's face expressed alarm.

" Do they make trouble for peaceable travelers ? "

" Sometimes they do, and sometimes they don't."

Uncle Charles rose to his feet.

" This—this is serious."

" Set down, Mister Dillin'ham, set down," said the old man, calmly. " Long as you're under my roof, you an' yours air in my keer, and I'd like to see the man that 'ud dare dispute it." His strong lower jaw, covered with thin, grizzly beard, set like iron, his light-colored eyes glittered dangerously. I felt the trustworthiness of his word, and I think Uncle Charles did, too, for he sank back into his chair with a partial sigh of relief.

Vague fears beset us; visions of hordes of lawless men swooping down upon us swept to

and fro through our minds. Alicia stole to her
father's side and sat down, and he took her
hand in his, and I nearly shrieked aloud when
one of the blacksmiths peered in at the door.
He was a small man with a sullen brow and
shifty eyes.

"Come in, Marcus, come in," said our host,
hospitably.

"I ain't got time this evenin'. I must be gittin' home."

"Got your wagon fixed?"

"Yes."

"An' them tools?"

"Yes, everything's done."

He disappeared.

Beasely was the name of our entertainers,
and early in the evening Mrs. Beasely proposed to show us to one of the little rooms.
Just as we were retiring, Uncle Ned came to
the front door again. He looked exceedingly
sheepish, and kept his eyes cast down, while
he said:

"I 'lowed I orter tell you 'bout Lightfoot."

" Yes ? "

" Dey found a stone under his shoe."

" Aha ! just as I supposed they would," I cried, triumphantly.

" Mighty myster'ous, dough, how it got dar," he muttered.

" Worked its way under, of course."

" It was put dar, honey — put dar by de power o' dem dat serves de debbil, an' dar'll be more trouble, too, 'fore we git out'n dese mountings," he said, earnestly.

I tried to make very light of that last asser-tion, but, remembering Mr. Beasely's words, my heart failed me.

When I went into our room, Nell lay half buried in the middle of the great feather-bed, but Alicia sat on a wooden chest only partly undressed.

" What do you think, Rachel ? " she whis-pered.

" That I may have to use this after all," I re-plied, drawing the pistol from my pocket with an air of bravado.

Nell instantly disappeared under the cover with a little cry of alarm.

"Put that thing up, Rachel; I don't want it going off here. You will kill one of us yet. What are you and Alicia whispering about?"

"Didn't you hear father and Mr. Beasely talking?" said Alicia.

"No, I didn't; I was asleep."

"Well, go to sleep again," I said, placing the pistol on the floor under the bed.

"I will, if you and Alicia can stop talking. Girls, it is perfectly heavenly to be on a real bed again, and not a made-up affair with a leaky tent over it."

We were very tired, and, in spite of our fears, Alicia and I were soon asleep. It was near twelve o'clock that I was awakened by Alicia clutching my arm, and calling me.

"Rachel! Rachel!"

"Yes," I muttered, sleepily.

"I hear strange voices."

"Where?" I whispered, starting up in bed, trembling with terror, but alert.

3

" In the yard; listen!"

I sprang up, and crept softly over the bare
floor to the front of the room. There were great
airy chinks between the rough logs of the wall,
and kneeling down I peered through one of
them. The clouds had broken, for fleeting
gleams of moonlight shone on the yard. The
furnace-fire in the blacksmith's shop was still
lighted, and I could see some of the negro men,
the field-hands, sitting around it. Not far from
the corner of the house two white men were
standing, talking in such low tones that I could
not catch the drift of their conversation. In a
few minutes a third man came up with a large
jug in his hand, and they moved away across
the yard. But they had not advanced many
steps before Mr. Beasely met them.

" What have you got thar, Jeems?" he demanded, sternly.

Sullen silence prevailed.

" You mought as well tell me at once, for you'll
not take another step until you do,"and the moonlight gleamed on the polished barrel of a gun.

"It's whiskey, pap."

"I 'lowed so. Takin' it to them niggers, air you?"

"They begged us for it: they're ready to pay."

"That don't make no difference. Didn't I tell you not to fetch a drop to anybody? You'd be a takin' them to the 'stillery, I reckon, if you dared. Don't you know that stuff 'ud make debils o' them? I told their marster he and hisn would be safe on this place, an' I mean to keep my word. You'll never ketch your pap a nappin' on duty, my son. Tote your whiskey back whar it came from."

They protested, they pleaded and blustered, but he could not be moved.

"Look a here, these people will git into trouble enough 'fore they leave the mountins, if they don't hurry, 'thout anything bein' done. Don't act like fools, or you'll have them conscriptin' officers on your track agin."

"That's jest it," exclaimed one of the men; "this fellow will be blabbin'."

"Hold your tongue. What does he know

'bout any o' you bein' deserters ? an' them gals
has about as much sense as a week-old baby.
Clear out, an' don't let me see hair or hide o'
any o' you agin to-night, or I'm mighty feered
somebody 'll git hurt."

He played with his gun in a very suggestive
way, and they reluctantly left him master of
the situation. He retreated to the fence and
sat down.

"It 'ud take a small army to outdo pap when
he gits his head sot," one of the young men
muttered, as they disappeared around the
house.

I felt such admiration for, and gratitude to,
the old man, that I longed to rush out and tell
him. His courage and honesty inspired me
with such trust, that, after reassuring Alicia,
who lay trembling under the bedclothes, I lay
down and slept soundly until morning.

CHAPTER III.

UNCLE CHARLES insisted on leaving several bright gold pieces in Mr. Beasely's hand when we departed next morning, and I bestowed half my jewelry on the girls. It was a clear day, and the brilliant sunshine dispelled my fears. I would not tell my uncle what I had overheard during the night, but urged him to travel as rapidly as possible. Nell and I once more took to the saddle, sometimes leading, sometimes following, the caravan.

It was late in the afternoon that we fell some distance behind, having stopped at a roadside spring for a drink of water, and to gather a handful of ferns, russet brown from the frost. A day of unmolested travel made us careless, and we lingered some time, robbing a Spanish oak of its scarlet foliage, to decorate our horses with. Then we walked leisurely along the road for a mile, before we mounted.

The sun was sinking below the western peaks, and the silence of the shadowy woods made us hasten on.

" What does that mean ?" Nell suddenly exclaimed, pointing her whip to a ridge ahead of us.

I looked, and grew pale, for on that ridge the highway forked, one road leading to the southwest, the other to the southeast.

" That is nothing; we can see them, of course, from that vantage-ground," I cried, and urged my tired Lightfoot into a gallop. We stopped at the forks of the road and looked to the right and the left, but not a glimpse of the caravan appeared. We examined the roads. Marks of recent travel appeared on both. The road to the left curved round the base of a mountain, and was quickly lost to view, but the one on the right kept more to the open valley for miles, its dull red surface appearing here and there where it crossed a ridge. I was inclined to take it, but Nell hesitated—held back.

"We cannot spend the night here!" I cried, between anger and despair.

"But if we take the wrong road?"

"We must risk that. Come."

"Oh, if we only *knew*," and she wrung her hands distractedly.

"Look! look!" I screamed, excitedly, pointing to one of those remote ridges. A white covered wagon was creeping slowly along the bit of road in view. For a moment it seemed to stand out on the crest of the hill, then vanished into the hollow beyond. We needed no further proof, and with a mixture of laughter and tears we dashed away fleet as the wind, in pursuit of that team. On and on we rode, until the valley was left behind, and we entered a defile of the mountains again, where the gloom of twilight reigned, without discovering our friends.

"I don't like this, Rachel," said Nell, looking fearfully around.

I didn't, either, but I had no intention of betraying my fears just yet.

"We will catch up with them in a few minutes," I said, hopefully. "You saw the wagon, Nell."

"Yes, but what has become of it?"

"They are driving fast to find a suitable camping-ground."

The way grew wilder. Mountains rose sharply on either side, broken here and there by gorges so deep that we shuddered as we plunged into them. We might have been in a primeval wilderness for all the signs of human life we could discover. The real twilight was casting its gloom about us, the strip of sky seen between the trees changing from blue to rose, under the flush of evening. I looked at Nell. Tears were streaming silently down her cheeks. I could not trust my voice to utter a word of consolation, knowing that if I did, I, too, would break into weeping, and even in the midst of my perplexity and terror the spectacle of two young women riding along the road crying like babies made me laugh hysterically.

We were passing through one of those terrible

ravines, terrible to us because peopled with a thousand imaginary dangers, when half a dozen men rode out before us. Nell screamed aloud, and I came near falling from my horse, so faint with fright did I become.

"The advance guard, eh?" said one of the men with a rude laugh. "Where are your teams?" he demanded.

"That is what we would like to know," I said in a trembling tone; and then I plucked up courage to explain our situation.

"Who knows that she is tellin' the truth, boys?" said a gruff, hard-faced fellow, eying me suspiciously. "Wimmen air precious liars, all of 'em."

"Indeed she tells the truth," sobbed my cousin piteously. "We saw a wagon in the distance and thought we were on the right road."

"Take 'em in hand, till we ketch up with the old man. Plenty o' bridle-trails across the country to the other road."

"How did you know—who told you we were coming?" I stammered faintly.

A cunning laugh greeted the question.
" News travels over this country fast, and
straight as a crow flies," said the rough com-
mander of the squad. " Come," he said, " we'll
do you no harm. We only want your money
and your niggers."

He laid his hand on Nell's bridle-rein, and
she screamed until a thousand weird echoes
answered from the mountains. " That's right,"
cried the man grimly, " make yourself hoarse
yellin', if you want to. It's all you can do, and
I s'pose it's some comfort. It ain't no use,
though. There's not a soul to hear you that'll
come to your help."

His brutal frankness swept away our last
hope. The courage of desperation whetted my
tongue to sharp words :

" I did not know that honest soldiers made
war on women."

" Maybe we don't claim to be honest soldiers.
We don't belong to neither side. We're inde-
pendents, fightin' for ourselves."

Common robbers ! My heart sank within

me. They wheeled into a settlement road, forc-
ing us to bear them company. Oh, that ride!
keen thrills of emotion dart through me now at
the memory of it. We rode through the woods,
darkness on every hand. Sometimes we passed
over the bed of a stream, then through thick
underbrush, cold wet leaves grazing our faces.
An icy vapor rose from the moist earth, my
hands ached with cold, my heart with dread.
Vague horrors oppressed me, as well as real
ones. In agony I thought of the dismay, the
utter distraction of Alicia and Uncle Charles,
the lamentations of the servants. I wondered
if I should ever again lay my head on Aunt
Milly's bosom. Tears burned my eyelids as I
recalled harsh words uttered to poor faithful old
Ned. I reproached myself, too, for desiring to
take the right-hand road; perhaps Nell would
have chosen the other, had I not been so over-
confident about the wagon, which proved to be
only a market wagon, I learned from one of
the men. Nell continued to weep, and I
pressed close to her.

"I take all the blame," I said, in a choked tone. "I saw you were inclined to the other road, but I thought my judgment best."

"We—we did wrong to stop so long at that spring. Where are they taking us?"

"Into the bowels of the earth, apparently," I whispered, as we descended into darkness so intense, it seemed to smite our eyes with sudden blindness. It grew lighter again, and in a few minutes we came out on a low ridge. We crossed it riding single file, and the sound of falling water penetrated the silence. It swelled to a roar as we advanced, the forest grew thinner, starlight prevaded the gloom with pale radiance. The road shelved down again, and before us rose a pile of buildings—an old saw-mill with a pond behind it, and a water-wheel. In the open ground before the mill a camp-fire still burned low, its glowing coals half covered with grey embers. Our captors halted, and we were told to dismount. A young fellow offered to assist Nell, but she sprang to the ground with such a haughty refusal of his services, that he fell back, abashed.

The fire was replenished with dry brush-wood brought from the mill, and we sat on a box near it. The men were not very rude nor very talkative. They went about, for the most part, grimly silent. They were rough, but not really disrespectful to us. An old man came out of the mill.

" Captain gone to bed ? " inquired one of the band, lighting a pipe.

" Yes, but he's gittin' up agin."

"How is he ?"

" Mendin' very fast, now. What er you all been up to ?" staring hard at us out of a pair of blinking, rheumy eyes.

" Tryin' to ketch a man who went t'other road."

" What for ? "

" To git his money and set his niggers free."

" Whar did these young wimmen come from ?"

" They're part o' the old man's property.

They lagged behind, and then tuk the wrong road at the forks."

The old man rubbed his hands together, the dry skin on them crackling as he did so, then he turned and went back into the mill. My dull eyes followed his bent figure, and I saw the yellow flickering glow of a candle as he opened the door. The creaking shutter closed behind him, but in a few minutes it opened again, and a far different figure appeared. My heart thrilled with expectation, with—I know not what feeling, when I recognized the blue uniform of a Union soldier. The flame of the camp-fire threw up the color in bold relief against the dark building, and also the man who wore it. He was young and had suffered recent illness. His clothes hung loosely on him, his face looked pinched and sunken. But the fire of his eyes ! What surprise and indignation it expressed ! He came straight to the camp-fire, took off his cloth cap to Nell and me, then turned to the men.

" What is the meaning of this story old Thur-

man has been telling me? Is it true that you
have been planning to rob—rob some travelers?
that these ladies were captured and brought
here by force?"

"Nobody has harmed 'em, captain. I wouldn't
touch a hair o' their heads," said the leader, in a
sullen tone, his weather-beaten face turning red.

"I thought you were honest men."

"We've treated you well, sir."

"So you have, my friend. You took me in,
and nursed me through a desperate fever; you've
sheltered and fed me; won my gratitude, my
heart, with your kindness—and to find you
thieves and robbers!"

He threw up his hand with such a gesture of
pain and contempt that it must have touched
every callous heart in the company.

"Fo'ks mustn't travel through this country
with a lot o' slaves, if they don't want to git in
trouble. We believe in freedom to all, we do."

"So do I, and it will come; it is coming.
Step back to the mill with me, and let us see if
we cannot settle this matter differently."

They all rose and followed him reluctantly, and we were left alone by the camp-fire.

" What do you suppose they intend to do with us, Rachel ? " Nell whispered, clinging to me.

" We are safe," I said, firmly. " He will protect us."

" How do you know ? "

" I cannot tell how I know it, but I *do* know it."

And he did. What arguments he used I knew not then, but presently the men came out, looking sullen, but ashamed and subdued. Two of them mounted horses and rode away: the others set about cooking supper. The soldier came back to us. I read victory on his brow, in his eyes—dominant, piercing eyes of dark gray—and the smile on his lips. He stood bare-headed before us—said:

" It has all been arranged. It will be best for you to remain here. Two of the men have gone to meet your friends, for they would naturally turn back to search for you."

I looked up, and eye met eye for a moment, and in that glance the last doubt perished.

"Believe me, you are safe," he said.

"I do believe it, sir," I replied, speaking to him for the first time.

Nell and I both felt that we ought to thank him, but he put aside our stammering speeches with some quiet inquiry about the day. The old man brought out a blanket, folded and spread it on the ground, and the soldier threw himself down on it, and I felt certain that he intended to remain near us until we were once more with our friends. He might be an enemy to our country—he was a true friend to us.

I left it to Nell to give a full explanation of our situation, and the causes leading to it. His eager attention flattered her; a sparkle of animation kindled in her tear-stained eyes; a flush rose to her young face. Her tumbled curls gave only a picturesque touch to her beauty, and a short, unworthy pang of envy smote my heart. The soldier looked at her, and I at him.

At first my glances were rather furtive, but,

4

as he seemed not to notice me, I grew bolder. His face interested, fascinated me: force of character, power lay behind it. His features were nobly cut, but his light hair and moustache contrasted oddly with his brown skin. One long, thin hand supported his head, and the firelight played caressingly over him. The rare glances he gave me seemed to pierce to the depths of my heart, rousing mysterious emotions.

I speculated on the probable mission bringing him, an officer in the Union army, to this remote region. Could he be a spy, penetrating the enemy's country for secret information? He wore his uniform boldly, but that he could safely do in the mountains.

When Nell finished her story, he knew a good deal about our family—where we had lived, and where we were going. He uttered an exclamation when she mentioned Decatur.

"Decatur, Georgia?" he asked, quickly, a strange expression on his face.

"Do you know the place?" I inquired.

"I—have been there," he said, and fell into sudden silence, his eyes fixed on the ground.

The mountaineers had baked some hoecakes, and broiled slices of bacon, and when we were offered a share of it we gladly accepted, being very hungry. As the night advanced we were so overcome with weariness that we consented to follow the old man Thurman into the mill, where he made up a bunk for us.

"But what will you do?" I said to the soldier, lingering a moment when he rose to bid us good-night.

"Remain here, Miss Douglas."

"Will it be safe to expose yourself to the night-air after your illness?"

He smiled, bending on me a look of mingled gratitude and pleasure.

"Thank you for your interest. It is most kind, but a soldier must be hardened to all changes of the weather."

* * * * *

A flash of lights, the tones of a familiar voice roused us.

" Father!" cried Nell.

I opened my eyes, and saw Uncle Charles bending over us, tears of relief and joy trickling down his bearded cheeks.

CHAPTER IV.

WE did not part from the gallant soldier until noon, next day, for he accompanied us back to the camp and several miles on our journey, as far, in fact, as it was safe for him to go in that uniform.

Uncle Charles did not scold us for our carelessness—he was too thankful to get us back again; but shame and self-reproach overcame us as he told the grief and dismay when we failed to appear after they went into camp. Certain that we had taken the wrong road, he and three trusty, stalwart negroes hastened back to search for us, leaving the camp in charge of Alicia and Uncle Ned. His gratitude to the brave Union officer was unbounded, and he longed to repay him in some way for his care of us.

" I must at least have the pleasure of know-

ing your name, and where you are from," he
said.

"Certainly, Mr. Dillingham; Arnold Lambert, from New York."

I will pass over our return journey to the
camp, and the extravagant joy manifested on
our arrival.

"How many of those highwaymen did you
shoot, Rachel?" Alicia inquired, between
laughter and tears, when she embraced me.

I had never so much as thought of my pistol.

I felt loth to part with Arnold Lambert when
he declared that he must turn back again. No
man had ever before so *interested* me, or appeared so heroic in my eyes. I knew nothing
about his life, his family ties, or the state of his
affections, whether bond or free. He preserved
a singular reticence about his own history or
affairs, but I knew him to be a gentleman, and
a strong, brave one.

Fearful that I should betray my feelings, I
held aloof, and he came last to me when bidding us good-bye. Did my eyes betray me

when he took my hand? his own kindled
warmly; he pressed my trembling fingers
closely.

" I am so grateful—so grateful ! " I murmured; " and if we never meet again—— "

" But we shall, we must, meet again," he
said, quickly.

" Oh, do you think so ? But this war—— "

" If you stop near Decatur I shall see you—
very soon."

I had no time to question him. He was on
his horse in a moment, waved us a last farewell, and turned away. But the sadness of
parting had left me. He had said we would
meet again very soon.

The remainder of our journey passed without
incident worthy to be chronicled. We were
glad when the end drew near. We passed
through Atlanta early one afternoon, avoiding
the more public streets, and turned into the
Decatur road. It was only a few miles to the
village, and just beyond it home awaited us..
We hurried over those last miles as rapidly as

the jaded horses could travel, and in a short
time were on the outskirts of the plantation.
Everybody felt more or less excited, but the
negroes were nearly beside themselves. The
news of our arrival had preceded us, and while
we were yet a full quarter of a mile away we
heard a murmur of human voices. At first it
was like a whisper on the silent air, but it
swelled tumultuously, swept over and around
us like the waves of a sea. In the distance a
cloud of dust rose from the road, and out of it
came a surging mass of humanity—the slaves
running to meet their friends. The strongest,
fleetest-footed led; the old and feeble tottered
in the rear.

With a great cry, those we had with us leaped to meet them; and such a meeting ! They
embraced, they wept, they shouted, and rent
their garments in excess of joy. Parents and
children, husbands and wives, brothers and
sisters were reunited. We stood aloof and
wept in sympathy, that great, overwhelming
joy bearing us away on its high flood-tide.

CHAPTER V.

WE had been at home two weeks; my uncle had picked up many of the broken threads of his life, and we verified a number of childish memories. Since Uncle Reuben's death the plantation had been in charge of young Reuben Howard, a distant cousin and namesake to Uncle Reuben. Cousin Reuben was a retiring, simple-minded little man, with a dignity of manner which did much for his insignificant physique. He was as refined and delicate in his tastes as a woman, and as honorable and chivalrous as the best example of a knight-errant. A cleaner-handed, whiter-souled gentleman than Cousin Reuben never lived. The slaves were devoted to him, and when he would have surrendered the reins of government to Uncle Charles, he wisely refused to take them.

"What! would you desert us, Reuben, the moment we arrive?"

" I have been thinking, sir, that, now my duties here are over, I would go into service," he said, quietly.

" You are not strong enough to endure the exposure and rough service of a soldier's life."

Reuben flushed sensitively.

" I know I am a weakling when it comes to physical strength, but the will is strong," lifting his eyes, aglow with the fire of an enthusiast. " Every man, young and old, will be needed before the struggle ends. I have hired a substitute, but—— "

" Don't go yet," said Alicia, sharp entreaty in her tone.

" No, no, not yet; we will talk of it next spring," her father added, with decision.

Reuben said no more, but went about his daily occupations in his usual quiet, faithful way. To have another man in the house afforded us great satisfaction. He soon fell as meekly under our sway as Uncle Charles, and was far more amiable in contributing to our amusement, escorting us to various social gatherings in the village and round about—our appearance in the community rousing the hospitable instincts of our neighbors, wellnigh extinguished in the anxieties and terrors of the war.

On that isolated North Carolina plantation we had seemed very remote from the war and its agitating influences. Some of our friends went away, girding on their swords as knights bound for a tournament. But in our old home the deep and tragic meaning of the struggle was revealed to us. The people around us lived in a fever of alternate hope and fear, agony and joy. Every movement of the armies, every battle fought, sent its subtle influence throughout the country. If the Confederates won a victory, it was proclaimed aloud from every house-top, and exulted over; if they lost, the sound of mourning filled the land. We caught the prevailing spirit, and outrebeled the deepest-dyed rebel of them all. We scraped linen for the hospitals, and, not finding as much old linen as we desired among our stores, sac-

rificed our dainty chemises and petticoats to
our loyal zeal. Alicia fell to knitting woolen
socks, while Nell and I spent half our time in
the spinning-room with the negro women, preparing thread for her. What piles of yarn we
dyed and wound! Years after, I found some
of those gray balls in the garret, dusty and
moth-eaten.

One Union soldier I could not forget—Arnold Lambert. At all hours of the day he
came into my thoughts, and even when most
ardent in my loyalty to our own soldiers, tenderness and pity for him penetrated my heart.
Occasionally Nell would mention his name,
but no one suspected my abiding interest in
him.

About three weeks after our arrival it was
rumored that we were to have amateur theatricals at the Decatur town-hall. A party of Atlanta ladies and gentlemen had formed a
troupe to play in various towns and cities
for the benefit of the soldiers—our soldiers.
Some of these amateurs were nearly as good

as professional actors and actresses, and they
had crowded houses wherever they went, not
only from a loyal desire on the part of the people to help the soldiers, but for the pleasure to
be derived from the entertainment. Nell and
I rode into the village one afternoon and saw
the first playbill stuck in a window. We visited the hall, where a stage was being erected,
and where we learned that a few local musicians were to contribute to the entertainment.
These people belonged to the village gentry,
and we had met them at certain parties. When
they invited us to help them out, I was delighted. Nell declined, but it was arranged that I
should sing some war ballads.

From that time I ceased to spin yarn or roll
linen, but went about singing, or drummed
for hours on the piano. Aunt Milly cut and
made a new gown for me—a white swiss, crisp
and full-skirted, the sleeveless bodice garnish-
ed with a wreath of artificial ivy leaves. Then
the day of the entertainment arrived, and I
went into the village to see about the final ar-

rangements. I went alone, and on horseback, and returned as the sun declined low in the west. It was Indian summer, and a violet haze hung over the fields and softened the brilliant autumn colors—the scarlet and yellow—of the woods. Only one house stood between my uncle's place and the village—a large old mansion in a grove of oaks. It was not directly on the public road, but a broad drive led up to the front gate, then curved around the fence and through a belt of timber to my uncle's. It was a short cut, and often traversed by us for that reason.

I remembered that house in my childhood as the old Montgomery place. The family had all died out or moved away, and the house fell into decay. When we came back we found that it had been renovated and sold to an Atlanta family, though the original name still clung to it. A considerable plantation lay back of it, but the Atlantians did not belong to the farming fraternity, and the land was rented to their neighbors. They merely came out of the city for the summer. The house had been shut up ever since our return, and sometimes in passing we stopped to gather a few of the roses blooming so abundantly in the front yard and in the garden.

That afternoon I turned out of the public road, intending to stop and pull a handful of the finest varieties for Alicia and Nell. As I rode up to the gate, I saw a man standing in the shadow of a crape-myrtle near it, his arms folded on the fence. He was in citizen's clothes, with a broad-brimmed soft hat pulled well over his face, and a gray military cloak thrown around his shoulders. He did not see me until I had drawn very near, then he drew back with a startled movement, looking full in my face. A violent trembling seized me in every limb: I went first white, then deeply red, my heart wellnigh choking me with its wild beating, for it was Captain Arnold Lambert.

He recognized me at the same moment, thrust open the gate, and stepped out with extended hand, and hat off.

" Captain Lambert!" I faltered.

"I told you that I should see you, Miss Douglas," smiling and looking at me with an expression in his eyes before which my heart thrilled, yet quailed.

"I did not expect it in this way. Is it not dangerous for you to be here?" with a sudden remembrance that he was not for, but against, us; that he would be hunted down and captured, if a breath of suspicion got abroad.

" Not unless you betray me."

"Don't speak of that, even in jest," I said warmly. " You are our friend, always our friend."

" May I indeed think so? Will you not change because I am one of the enemy?"

He spoke earnestly, sadly, resting his hand on the horn of my saddle, his eyes raised to mine.

" I wish it were different, that you were one of us, but I can never regard you as an enemy, never."

" An enemy to you? I should think not!" he exclaimed.

Lightfoot pawed the ground impatiently and

made a step forward. I suddenly dismounted
and threw the bridle over my arm.

"Are you a friend to the people who own
this place, Captain Lambert?"

"I—once knew them."

"The house is closed, the grounds deserted.
We stop sometimes to gather a few of the
lovely roses—do you think they would care if
they knew?"

"I know they would not. Come into the
garden with me," he said, eagerly. He looped
Lightfoot's bridle over the gate-post, and we
entered the yard. We walked slowly around
the house and into the garden. A broad walk
divided it down the centre, one-half of the
ground containing dried herbs and the dead
stalks of vegetables, the other filled with withered flowers. We went down the walk side by
side, and I tried to make clear the reality of it
to my mind, but it seemed dreamlike. I stole
as many glances as I dared at my companion.
He looked strong, well, and handsome, but
grave, so grave.

5

"Have you fully recovered your health?" I softly inquired.

"Yes, thank you; it was only a fever. Will you have some of these?" pausing and touching a rose-bush on which a few late scarlet buds still lingered.

"Yes, please."

What a delicious half-hour it was to me, walking about that old garden with Arnold Lambert, listening dreamily to the sound of his voice, meeting his kind, soft glances! The sun went down, pungent odors rose from the moist earth, a frosty chill pierced the air. Captain Lambert would have cut every rose in the garden, but I protested against it—entreated so earnestly that he stopped. I had told him about the entertainment, and that I should sing. I blushed as I betrayed that vanity, but he did not seem amused.

"Must you go now?" he said, as I moved again toward the gate.

"It is growing late, and you are to go with me. Uncle Charles—my cousins, will be very glad to see you."

"I thank you very much, but I leave this part of the country again to-night."

" You can at least take supper with us ? "

" Miss Douglas, it would not be safe."

The implied doubt of our good faith cut me to the heart.

"Do you think we would betray you ? " I said, in a choked tone, pain and anger struggling, each, for the mastery over me.

"God forbid ! Such a mean doubt I could not entertain ! " he cried. " You misunderstand me; but think if others should come in, of the servants, even. Do you think I would hesitate, otherwise ? No, no."

I was appeased, and begged him not to go beyond the gate with me, trembling for his safety the moment I knew he considered it wise to keep aloof from people, but he walked up that shadowy drive through the woods with me. He led my horse, I carried the roses, their fragrance spreading about us. We stepped slowly along, but talked hurriedly, as people conscious of being pressed for time. Once he said:

"Should a man follow duty under all circumstances?"

"*I* believe so," I said, unhesitatingly, as the
ignorant often speak.

"But if, to do so, he must sacrifice his home,
his kindred, love — everything most dear to
him?"

"He will be all the nobler."

He turned, looked searchingly into my face,
then glanced backward at the silent house we
were leaving. I felt some mystery underlay
his words, but refrained from questioning him
too closely.

"You are troubled," I said, softly.

"I am," he acknowledged, and sighed heavily.

"Can I help you?"

"No, your sympathy would be sweet. Beyond that no one can help me." He turned
again toward me, a smile banishing the gloom
from his face. The stern lines of his features
melted to tenderness, his eyes softened mar-
velously. Was it for me alone, or only a trib-
ute to all women? "Thank you for this half-

hour. I shall carry the memory of it back to camp with me."

"Shall I tell any one that I have seen you?"

"Do as you think best. I trust you fully."

"You—you really leave to-night?"

"Yes, my leave has expired."

I looked at him through the gathering dusk, and knew that it was more than friendship which had drawn us together. His eyes dwelt on me lingeringly—I felt that I could not part from him.

"This is really farewell, then?" I said, as steadily as I could.

"Not if I live, and you do not forbid me to come again." His glance fell on the rose I had fastened in the breast of my habit. "Give it to me as a token that I may come again."

With trembling fingers I loosened it and laid it in his hand. It was our farewell. He assisted me to mount, and raised his hat and bowed as I rode by. I would not look back, for fear he might see the tears on my cheeks. Just why I

wept I could scarcely tell. It seemed somewhat in pity for myself, for him, and for the
sadness over all the country.

I did not tell any one at home that I had
seen him.

CHAPTER VI.

WE had a full audience at the hall that night, though it seemed strange to see so few young men in the gathering. Here and there could be seen a gray uniform, but old men—planters— with their wives and daughters, and the village people, made up the audience. Around the doors crowds of boys had collected. I was introduced to the members of the Atlanta Company when I went behind the scenes, and very cordially greeted. As only a few of them appear in this chronicle it is unnecessary to say very much about them.

Mr. and Mrs. Ladislaw and Elinor Sims were the ones who interested me most deeply on first sight. He was a big, genial-looking man with a rich bass voice, and the gift of inspiring the faintest-hearted and most cowardly with confidence and nerve. He managed the whole

troupe, and did it as no other man could, be-
sides sustaining a brilliant part on the stage.
His resources were varied, his tongue ever
ready. That subtle power we call personal
magnetism he possessed to a wonderful degree.
He was a good actor and a good musician. He
could improvise beautifully and sing with such
thrilling expression and effect that he could
move an audience to laughter or to tears with
the greatest ease. He had the voice and the
dramatic ability to become a famous singer, but
a different fate was in store for him.

Mary Ladislaw was a delicate-looking, rather
quiet woman, but plenty of endurance and nervous force lay under that subdued exterior.
She was thoroughly in sympathy with her husband. They had no children, so she devoted
herself to him and the Confederate soldiers.
They were her children and her heroes, and
for them she would have worked like a slave.
She was passionately loyal, but not bitter. Her
nature was too tender and sympathetic for ran-
cor to find lodgment in it. Poor Mary Ladislaw!

I did not learn all this in that first evening. It was after intimate acquaintance that I learned to know those two so well.

Elinor Sims was a girl a year or two older than myself. She was tall and rather proud-looking, but really very approachable and friendly. All Southern men and women who were true to the Rebel cause were brothers and sisters in those days. Strangers soon became intimate friends, bound together by a common interest. Miss Sims and I sat on a box behind the scenes and talked in a frank and friendly spirit. When she went on the stage I watched her from the wing, admiring her attitudes and gestures intensely. Her acting was both spirited and natural, and I felt that my country training had not prepared me to take any part in plays. I knew nothing of amateur theatricals beyond the simple, old-fashioned charades suitable for the parlor. They played a little drama adapted from an old French play, and it was both pathetic and humorous. There was a paucity of scenery, and

the curtain sometimes refused to come down at
the right moment, but the delighted audience
did not pay the slightest attention to those little
drawbacks.

Between the first and second acts I was called
upon to sing.   The actors had changes to make
in their toilettes, and some new scenery had to
be arranged.   Mr. Ladislaw led me out before
the curtain, then disappeared. I had never sung
before a larger audience than a parlor full of
people, and to meet the gaze of so many unfamiliar eyes made me palpitate with fear. But
the sight of the anxious, doubtful faces of my
relatives restored composure, and without accompaniment I began singing that dolorous
ballad called " Lorena."   It was very popular
at that time with soldier and civilian, and was
sung even in the negro cabins.   The hearts of
the people were easily touched, and silence fell
upon my audience as I warbled about the woes
of " Lorena," throwing all the tenderness and
expression that I could into my voice.   I really
felt a good deal of it.   I had been deeply dis-

turbed by that meeting with Captain Lambert and the way we had parted. My thoughts dwelt constantly on the uncertainties of a soldier's life, and the song affected me to tears, though I kept my voice steady. My emotion communicated itself to the audience, and a few melancholy, hysterical women wept aloud in a gentle way.

I do not like to think now how lackadaisical I must have looked, but the sentiment seemed to suit the time and people. Loud applause followed me when I withdrew behind the curtain. Mr. Ladislaw hurried to me.

" It was very successful, very," he said heartily. " You have made a hit."

" I acted like a simpleton," I said, the sentimental mood already passing away.

" Oh, no. You sang with feeling, with fine expression. We must have you in our troupe. We are not quite ready for the second act. Our scenery insists on falling to pieces, and some of the costumes have gone astray. Will you not go on and sing something else?"

"Do, Miss Douglas," cried Mrs. Ladislaw, coming out of a dressing-room with her mouth full of pins and a long silk gown over her arm. "Elinor has lost her wig and we must powder the old one."

Flattered by the appreciation of the audience, and feeling that I could really be of service by filling up the time, I went back on the stage blushing and courtesying. As I raised my eyes they fell on a tall gray-cloaked figure standing back in shadow near the door, and I recognized Captain Lambert. Dizziness came over me. I caught my breath in a gasp, feeling only extreme terror that he should so recklessly expose himself to detection and capture. His black broad-brimmed hat shielded his face, and when I had time to observe that no one paid the slightest attention to him, my courage revived. His presence soothed, yet agitated me. I was conscious of a feeling of satisfaction that he should see me in evening dress, and looking my bravest and best, even in the midst of a tumult of other emotions. How I longed

to stretch out my hands across that throng to
him ! The words of an old ballad, learned from
my mother in childhood, came back to my
memory, and, looking at that motionless figure,
feeling the influence of the eyes watching me
from under that disguising hat, I sang:

> " ' Farewell, farewell,' is a lonely sound
>   And often brings a sigh;
>   But the heart feels most when the lips move not
>   And the eyes speak a gentle ' good-bye.'

> " ' Adieu, adieu,' will do for the gay
>   When pleasure's throng is nigh;
>   But give to me that better word
>   That comes from the heart, ' good-bye.' "

The curtain, after various hitches, had gone
down for the last time, and actors and audience
mingled in a social half-hour's talk. Uncle
Charles, beaming with hospitality, went about
asking various members of the troupe to become his guests for the night, and he secured
one of the gentlemen. I wandered about in a
fever of excitement, wondering if Captain Lam-

bert still lingered in the hall, yet not daring to
go near the door for fear of betraying him.
Miss Sims and I were standing together when
she missed her brooch.

" I will go behind the scenes and look for it,"
I said, eager to get away to myself a few
minutes.

" I will go with you.   I had it while dressing.
It must be with my things."

We ran up to the stage and vanished behind
the curtain.   A ghostly twilight reigned, the
white sheets dividing the dressing-rooms swaying to and fro.   Hampers of stage-clothing
were scattered about the floor; tin swords, de-
canters, and drinking-cups were thrown carelessly together.   A passage-way opened between the dressing-rooms, and we were entering
it, Miss Sims a little in advance, when a man
stepped out before us.   He did not see me, or,
seeing, did not recognize me, muffled in cloak
and hood.   His eyes were on Miss Sims; he
held out his hands to her.

" Dear Elinor ! "

"*Arnold!*" she cried, fear, doubt, passionate joy in her tone. She threw her arms about him, her face against his shoulder.

I silently retreated, leaving them alone.

CHAPTER VII.

THINK you I slept that night? Not enough for the most fleeting dream. All the way home my cousins talked of the play and the players, appealing to me when they failed to be satisfied with their own opinions. I gave only random replies. Their cheerful voices, their arguments over trivial details, tortured me. Why could they not divine my feelings, and keep silent, or at least not expect me to join in the conversation? Yet, had they suspected the state of my mind, I would have been covered with shame.

"What is the matter, Rachel? are you sleepy?" inquired Alicia, when I merely muttered a reply to some question she asked.

"She is so puffed up with pride over her success this evening that she cannot any longer notice common folks," said Nell, mockingly.

"Perhaps Rachel is thinking of joining this company," said Cousin Reuben's gentle voice.

"Yes, I am," I said hastily, heedlessly catching at the suggestion.

Consternation held my cousins silent for a few minutes, then a perfect avalanche of exclamations and questions poured upon me.

As we passed the old Montgomery place I pressed my face against the carriage window, but darkness hid all except the outlines of the house from my gaze. I thought of the garden lying cold and deserted, the rose-bushes stripped of their last lovely blooms. Pain and rage convulsed me; I hated Captain Lambert at that moment. When we reached home the carriage was sent back for my uncle and his guest, who had to stay at the hall long enough to pack his stage wardrobe. I fled to my room, but there encountered my two old servants, who were sitting up for me. Uncle Ned laid fresh logs on the fire, and snuffed the candles, while Aunt Milly took off my wraps.

6

" Honey, you do look mighty pale," she exclaimed anxiously.

"I 'spect she tuk a chill in dem t'in no-
count clo'es," said old Ned, eying my bare
neck and arms with disapproval. "Did you
have a good time, Miss Rachel, honey?"

"Yes—no—I cannot tell you to-night, Uncle
Ned."

"Don't you see she's wore out an' sleepy?
Go 'long, Ned, an' don't ax no more questions,"
said Aunt Milly, sharply.

He shuffled reluctantly to the door.

"I 'spect you *is* tired, Miss Rachel?"

"I am," I said, absently.

He went out and closed the door.

"Now, honey, you gwine to git in bed, and
kivered up dis minute. Dese arms o' yourn
feel lack dey'd been fros'bitten," said Aunt
Milly, imperiously.

I submitted passively to her nimble old fingers, knowing that it would be the best way to
get rid of her, and she soon had my finery off,
and my hair brushed. I crept into the soft,

high bed, and she tucked the white, chilly sheets around me, smoothing and patting the pillows until they were arranged to her satisfaction. I watched her as she moved softly about the room, setting it in order, muttering and nodding her turbaned head, as she noted the creases in my new gown. Finally she put out the candles, and disappeared. The moment she closed the door, I flung off the covering, and got out of bed. At last I was alone, and could beat my breast, or writhe and weep in impotent rage or anguish. While driving home it had seemed to me that I must give some vent to my feelings, or perish; yet, now that the necessity for self-control had been removed, I no longer felt any desire to weep. The violence of my emotion had spent itself; only a dull sense of loss and pain made my heart ache.

My thoughts were clear, quickened by the smart of wounded pride; all the faculties of my mind seemed unusually alert and active.

I sat down before the fire, and reviewed every moment of my acquaintance with Arnold

Lambert, every word he had said to me, every glance given. I could not believe him capable of any desire to trifle with me. Such a doubt seemed so unworthy of him and of myself that I rejected it at once. I had simply misunderstood his advances, believed him in love with me, when he merely felt a friendly interest. Vanity, and my own tenderness of heart toward him, had led me astray. To acknowledge that as the true explanation was the most bitter and humiliating experience of my hitherto superficial life. To recognize myself as a woman loving, but unloved, smote my pride to the quick, for I did love him—I knew it by every pang I suffered.

No wonder he was troubled as he walked in that garden with me. He, was thinking of Elinor Sims. He had talked to me simply because he craved sympathy, and chance had thrown me in his way. I could not but pity those lovers, separated by such diverse opinions: one loyal to the Union, the other bound to the Confederate cause. Sympathy and jeal-

ousy each struggled for the mastery over me,
as I recalled that unexpected meeting behind
the stage. It was for a glimpse of her that he
exposed himself to the danger of recognition.
I cowered in the chair, and hid my face. How
I had poured out my heart to him in that song!

I am conscious how incoherent this part of
my story is, but I cannot, even now, recall the
thoughts and impressions of that night with
any clearness of recollection. They seemed
vivid enough at the time, but afterward became
merely a series of keen sensations.

I dwell on the experience because it changed
my life. Instead of dreaming dreams over the
old romances of poets and novelists, I henceforth
lived realities. I struck down into depths of nature hitherto unknown to me, and came up with
clearer views and steadier purpose. The careless girl no longer existed. A resolute woman
had replaced her.

The firelight faded; gray ashes covered the
dying coals. The room grew chilly; a pale
beam from the rising moon shone across the

floor. I had never been up so late alone, and the silence of the house impressed me with its likeness to death. I went back to bed, but not to sleep. It seemed to me that I could never sleep again until I had planned my future. To live quietly on in my uncle's house seemed impossible. I must turn my back on idleness and ease, if I would conquer myself. I thought of those amateur actors, of their self-sacrifices and hard work. I resolved to join them if they would accept my services. But could I meet Elinor Sims day after day, be thrown into intimate relations with her, and not become unjustly bitter in my feelings? The experiment would do no harm.

I went down to breakfast next morning quite strong and composed, upheld by my new resolutions. A bath and a turn in the open air had removed all trace of the sleepless night, but I felt so changed inwardly, I wondered that no one observed it in my face. Our guest proved to be a very agreeable young man from New Orleans, an officer in the Confederate service.

He had been wounded, and while on furlough
identified himself with the Amateurs, composing
music for them, and extracting a good deal of
pleasure out of the social life gathered about
them. Lieutenant Devreau was of French
descent, and a brave-spirited young fellow.
My cousin Nell coquetted with him at the
breakfast-table, and when the meal was over
they strolled into the garden. I followed Uncle
Charles to his study, and without any preamble
made known my desire to join the Amateurs.
He refused to listen to me, at first.

" You have as great a thirst for adventure as
a boy, Rachel; I thought your experiences in
the mountains would satisfy you."

"On the contrary, they created a desire for
more."

"It is not proper for a young woman to be
gadding about the world unprotected."

" I can have a companion."

"Are you displeased with your home,
child?"

" Oh, no ! " I cried.

"Then be contented to remain in it. You can find plenty to do."

"For my country?"

"Your country will not miss your services," smiling slightly.

His determined opposition only settled me more strongly in my purpose to leave. I argued and pleaded, but he held out against me. Then in despair I resolved to take him partly into my confidence. I approached his chair, leaned over his shoulder, and, in a low tone, said:

"I—I must go, Uncle Charles. I need a change—the opportunity to forget."

"Eh? What? Forget? Do you mean to say that—that you are in love?" wheeling around to stare at my burning face, the last word uttered in a shocked whisper.

I bowed in mute assent. He started up. "But—but this will never do. Who is it? Where does he live? Gad, Rachel! why don't you marry him?"

I grew more and more scarlet, regretting that I had betrayed myself to him.

"He does not love me."

"*Oh!* Well, well! I'd make him love you, if I could. My dear Rachel, my poor child." He pulled his beard unmercifully in his distress. "You shall go to-day, if you wish. I'll arrange it with the Ladislaws. Nice woman, don't you think so? Kind and sympathetic."

"If you say a word to her, Uncle Charles——"

"Oh, certainly not, if you don't wish me. You are looking pale this morning. Now don't fret yourself any more. No man is worth a sigh or a tear. I'm afraid I've been a poor guardian, a poor guardian to you, Rachel."

I could not forbear smiling.

"Dear Uncle Charles, you can guard my property and my person, but my heart—well, I think that is beyond your control."

"I suppose it is. Does he—does he live here? or is it somebody——"

"Please don't ask me," I cried, entreatingly.

"I won't, then; there, there, it doesn't make any difference where he lives, or what his name is. He is a fool not to love you, Rachel—an

imbecile; that is all I have got to say about
it."

I had no idea my uncle would take so much
interest in the matter. I knew he believed it
to be the duty, the sacred duty, of every woman
to marry. We had been brought up in that
faith, as it were, and he often hinted that Alicia
and I were letting our best chances slip by remaining single beyond the age of twenty-one,
but I did not realize that he would feel so
warmly over the state of my heart. I was embarrassed and distressed. It was plain that he
would like to proclaim the state of my affections from the house-top, pointing a finger of
scorn and derision at the foolish man who did
not love me. He wanted to tell him what he
thought of him—hold him up to the ridicule of
the country. I then and there decided that an
elderly guardian and relative was not the one
for a girl to confide her sentimental secrets to,
and I have not yet had cause to change my
mind.

It was a week before I left home, and during

that time Uncle Charles kept me in a state of constant terror with his solicitude and thinly veiled sympathy.

" What dark secrets are you and father keeping between you ? " Nell inquired.

" Secrets, Nell ! what nonsense ! " he exclaimed hastily, looking provokingly guilty. " I am only anxious about—about Rachel's health.''

She stared incredulously at me, and I blushed scarlet with vexation.

" Her health ? " she said, deliberately. " I never saw Rachel looking better. Are you wasting away inwardly, my dear girl ? "

" I wish you would leave me alone," I exclaimed, angrily, and left the room.

But all heartburning and annoyance had passed away the morning I bade my relatives good-bye and set my face toward a broader life, more stirring scenes. We traveled to Atlanta in a private conveyance. My two old servants accompanied me, and Uncle Charles did not leave me until he saw me comfortably

established in the same house with the Ladislaws.   My suite of rooms came next to theirs,
and they promised to protect and watch over
me as long as I should remain with them.

That evening I went to the rehearsal of
"The Soldier's Wife," a play written for the
Amateurs. I was given a small part in it—one
where no speaking was required—and felt that
I was fairly launched on my new career.

CHAPTER VIII.

THE only theatre in Atlanta at that time was the Athenæum. It was small, had no private boxes, and the stage was rather deficient in scenery. But it was the first real theatre I had ever entered, and the drop-curtain and scenic effects looked rather splendid in my rustic eyes. The rehearsal took place at the theatre, a few friends of the players sitting in the dimly lighted auditorium until it was over. "The Soldier's Wife" has, doubtless, long since been forgotten, except by a few; but it was a drama exactly suited to the time and circumstances, therefore very popular. It was full of pathetic scenes, and appealed strongly to the emotional side of one's nature. I remember that war-hardened soldiers wept over it, but the mercurial Southern temperament is

subject to quick changes from mirth to grief,
then back to mirth again.

My heart throbbed with excitement at the
thought of meeting Elinor Sims again. I wondered what she would say to me, and decided,
through a mixture of pique and generosity,
that she should not explain that meeting with
Captain Lambert. It would save her the embarrassment of telling me what I already
knew—that he was her lover—and also save me
the pain of hearing that acknowledgment. On
my part she should never know that I had met
him, unless he told her.

She met me with heightened color, and, as
soon as the ordinary words of greeting were
over, referred to that night in Decatur.

" You—why did you withdraw so quickly?
I wanted to introduce you to—Captain Lambert.
It was such a surprise to me to see him there,
and he—— "

" Please do not tell me about it," I hastily
interrupted her to say.

" We had only a few minutes together."

"I know."

"You—have heard?"

"Yes, yes; all that I wish to know," I said, with unintentional rudeness.

She flushed and bit her lip, evidently wounded, then walked away. I followed her.

"I beg your pardon," I said, gently; "I did not intend to speak so bluntly; I only wanted to save you the pain of explaining to a stranger, and—and—— "

"I understand how you feel," she said, sadly; and we dropped the subject, never to refer to it again, though we became very good friends.

She lived in the city with her grandfather and widowed mother, and I heard that she had a brother—Lieutenant Edgar Sims—in the army.

From this point my life seemed to suddenly broaden, like a full stream finding an outlet. I was enthusiastically interested in the work of the Amateurs, and, for the sake of aiding them all that I could, hired a music teacher, devoting several hours a day to practice. I also

learned to value the possession of money. It
had always come as a matter of course to me
to live in ease and have my servants. I did not
think about it, and the word " poverty " held
no special meaning for me; but when I realized
the suffering of the soldiers, and saw in many
instances the destitution of their families, I felt
like giving away all I possessed. I drew so
heavily on Uncle Charles that he came up to
Atlanta in alarm, to see how I spent so much
money.

Mrs. Ladislaw promised to look more carefully after my expenditures, and when he went
away she came into my room to caution me
against too lavish a charity:

" Give all that you can without impoverish-
ing yourself. If you become destitute you will
be an object of charity yourself. You cannot
work. You have never been trained to any
bread-winning trade."

" But if the war goes against us, if we are
defeated, it will be work then, will it not ? " I
said.

"I do not know; time enough to think of that."

"And look at this."

I seized the latest issue of the *Intelligencer*, the principal Atlanta paper, and spread it before her, pointing out certain appeals to the wealthy people of the city—of the whole country—to come to the relief of the half-naked, half-starved soldiers, fighting on the northern frontiers.

Her sensitive lip quivered with pain; she averted her eyes from the paper.

"I know it is hard to close one's hand against such pitiful needs."

"You do not close yours," I said, softly: "you give all that you have—money, time, love. Let me do the same."

"You are a rebel after my own heart, Rachel; but I fear that if you do not restrain this generous spirit your uncle will take you away from us."

That alarmed me, and I reluctantly promised to be more careful; but my pockets were stuff-

7

ed with crisp new Confederate bills, and when she went away I put on my bonnet and mantilla, and calling my servants went out through the city to distribute the money. My charity was not all pure generosity. I don't think I should have given away gold so lavishly, but a few far-seeing men had said that the day would come when Confederate money would not be worth the paper it was printed on. To keep it seemed foolish to me, then; particularly as it brought immediate relief to those in need.

I never went out alone. If I did not go with some of my new friends, Uncle Ned and Aunt Milly accompanied me, pacing solemnly along at a respectful distance in the rear. We often visited the hospitals, but they could never overcome their terror at the sight of dead or wounded men. " Miss Rachel, honey, dis ain't no place for you. Come away, for de Lawd's sake," they would plead, hovering around the door, unwilling to enter, but more unwilling that I should go in alone. Often I

had to cover my face with my mantle to shut
out some harrowing sight—a ghastly face,
drawn with intense suffering; a mutilated body
writhing convulsively—but my nerves were unusually strong for a delicately nurtured young
woman, and the pleasure my visits gave those
poor, brave fellows, lingering on the outer verge
of life, gave me courage. Afterward I put
that training to better service.

In strange contrast to these hospital scenes
were the evenings spent at the theatre, playing
my little part in "The Soldier's Wife," and
singing war ballads between the acts; or, if not
at the theatre, then in some parlor where social
life still ran gaily on the surface, and men and
women met in brave attire.

The war was always the chief topic of conversation at these social gatherings, and any
one who could bring the latest news from camp
was made a hero.

The Amateurs were going on a little tour in
December, and a few days before their departure they were given a reception and ball by

one of the wealthiest families in the city. Never had I looked on so brilliant a scene. Our country dances were insignificant in comparison. The house was brilliantly illuminated, and fragrant with flowers. Officers in uniform mingled with the more soberly clad civilians, and the women, young and old, were in their best apparel. Few grave faces were present. Pleasure, wit, gaiety, reigned, on the surface at least. It seemed that for a few hours, if no more, everybody had determined to throw off the gloom and fear brooding over the country. Spirits held in sad subjection cast off their fetters; eyes familiar with tears flashed brilliantly; lips used to sighs curved in laughter. We danced with unwearied feet.

The night was waning. Supper was over and the last set had formed a stately Virginia reel. The musicians were playing a few introductory strains, when the slow, steady tramp of weary feet sounded on the pavement outside, and " Maryland, My Maryland," sung by manly voices grown faint from hunger and fatigue,

penetrated the warm, fragrant rooms. Silence
fell upon the company. The dance music
ceased, and men and women crowded to the
doors and windows. It was only a company
returning from some hard campaign. Their
clothes were in rags: they marched slowly, too
footsore and worn to make much progress. At
last they were gone. Only the tread of a solitary sentinel made active life in the street, but
through the air still pulsed the sorrowful strains
of "Maryland, My Maryland," sung in husky
undertones.

A hand fell on my shoulder. I turned and
looked into Mary Ladislaw's eyes, dim with tears.

"Oh, the poor fellows, the brave heroes! and
we were trying to forget them. Come away,
Rachel."

I snatched the roses from my breast and
threw them to the ground.

"I will never dance again while this cruel
war lasts," I said, in choking tones.

The lights looked dim, the flowers withered.
In silence the company dispersed.

CHAPTER IX.

OF that tour I hold some very pleasant recollections. Everywhere the Amateurs played to full and appreciative audiences, and we were entertained in the most hospitable manner. The fact that it was a charitable organization, working for the soldiery of the country, opened the most tightly closed purses. We played in Augusta, Charleston, and all the principal towns along the route.

Mr. Ladislaw, always the moving spirit, the universal genius of the company, would rarely have two programmes alike. He was remarkably gifted in the quickness and grace with which he could turn the simplest prose into rhyme, and no more gratifying thing could he do than to sing the telegraphic reports from the army as they came in. It was a novel way to announce the progress of a battle, our vic-

tories or defeats. I've seen an audience sit in
breathless silence during one of those musical
recitals and then bring down the roof, almost,
with applause if the tidings were glad, or groan
and weep if they were sorrowful. He was always in communication with the various armies,
and often, during an engagement, telegrams
were brought to the theatre or hall to him. A
victory he sang in glad triumphant strains, a
defeat in minor tones.

We have sat behind the scenes and trembled
and cried with grief or joy under the influence
of his singing, as much as the audience.

Lieutenant Devreau had obtained a longer
leave from his post, and traveled with us. Before we left Atlanta I knew that Elinor Sims
was the attraction keeping him with the Amateurs, but his devotion became very evident
while we were on the road. It did not surprise
me that he should fall in love with her, but I
was surprised and indignant at the encouragement she gave him. I tried to think that it was
nothing to me; that if Arnold Lambert could

not take care of his own interests, it was not
my place to interfere. But her faithlessness
roused mingled feelings of contempt and satisfaction in my heart. It gave me a kind of
pleasure to think how much truer I was to him—
I, who had never won his love—than she who
had pledged her word.

I held as much aloof from her as circumstances would permit, and grew so cold in manner that she noticed it. She was of a frank and
tender nature, and, fearing that she had unwittingly offended me, came to me apart one evening and said :

"Are you angry with me, Rachel ?"

The question so sweetly and kindly asked
confused me. I blushed and hung my head
like a culprit, instead of holding it high in conscious rectitude while I read her a lecture on
the faithlessness of her conduct.

"Oh, no; why do you think so ? "

"You have been so cold and silent."

"You must be mistaken."

"I think I am, now," laughing. "We are

egotistical creatures. I have been fancying
that you were offended with me, when you
have been simply absorbed in your own affairs,
and not giving me a thought."

If I had only met her frankness half way, but
I was too cowardly. I had closed her confidences to me about Captain Lambert, and it
seemed impossible for me to mention his name
to her now. It would be taking a liberty, and
then I feared to betray my own interest in him.
It is so much easier at times to play the hypo-
crite than to speak the truth to our friends that
I think we are all more or less tempted to that
course. We often call this silence charity, when
it concerns the faults of others, and plume ourselves on being so generous, when, in reality,
our feelings are the reverse of generous.

I no longer held aloof from Elinor, but I continued to feel secretly bitter and contemptuous
toward her, while I pitied Lieutenant Devreau.
He was chivalrous and highly honorable, and
had the utmost faith in her. His ideas of women
were rather strict and frankly expressed. I

often heard him say that the smallest breach of faith in a woman was unpardonable. He thought women should be as exact and straightforward as men, and to excuse deceit or carelessness in them as amusing little weaknesses would be impossible for him.

Elinor would heartily agree with him, not even so much as changing color over her own duplicity. Her power of concealment amazed me. Did she feel so secure, or so conscience-less? Sometimes I was half tempted to regard that meeting of hers with Arnold Lambert as a phantasm of my own mind, but I had seen her in his arms, had heard him call her name in a passionately tender tone. I did not intend to play the spy on Elinor and her new lover, but when in their presence, my eyes seemed sharp-ened to such keenness of vision, all my senses were so alert, that I could not help seeing and understanding even the swiftest glances ex-changed between them.

Under any other circumstances I should have felt the keenest delight in this love-affair, but as it was, it kept me in a state of suppressed rage and disgust.

We were in Augusta when the summons for him to return to his duties in the army came. It was not time for the play to begin and he walked across the deserted stage with the crumpled telegram in his hand. I stood in the wing, a long cloak covering my evening dress. The lights were turned very low, but as he approached me I read the evil tidings in his downcast face and dejected walk. I pitied him.

" Miss Douglas, has Miss Sims arrived yet ?" he inquired.

"She is in the dressing-room. Shall I call her?"

" Thank you, please do; I must go away in an hour."

" Leave us ? "

" Yes," sighing heavily. " I have neglected my duty too long as it is."

I met Elinor coming from the dressing-room. Lieutenant Devreau had followed me, and glancing over my shoulder she was startled at the look upon his face. Her cheeks paled under their stage paint and powder; dread flashed into her eyes.

"What is the matter, Royal?" she faltered.

"Can you not guess, my darling? I must leave to-night, within an hour, for camp again. I ought to have gone a month ago."

Neither of them seemed to heed my presence. He drew her back within the shadow of the scenery, his arms about her.

"If we could only be married before I go," he said, in trembling tones. "You would not refuse if you were at home, would you, Elinor?"

"No, no," she whispered.

"My own dear love!"

The murmur of their voices followed me as I stole away. I wondered, bitterly, if she remembered that interview with Captain Lambert in the Decatur town-hall.

She was a strong, brave girl. She bade her lover good-bye, dried her eyes, and played her part that evening as brilliantly as ever. I watched her closely and could but acknowledge that she won my reluctant admiration.

CHAPTER X.

IT was in February that I returned home on
a visit. To realize the changes wrought by contact with the world, and travel, it is necessary
to return to the familiar surroundings of one's
former life. The months of my absence were
so crowded with experiences they were like
years to me, but they might have passed as one
day in my uncle's household. Nothing on the
plantation had visibly changed except the season. The field-hands went out to their work
at dawn, clearing new land and breaking up
the old soil, preparing to plant the crops. The
house-women spent the days in the workroom
spinning and weaving, and teaching the older
children, who were to become house-servants,
how to sew. It was all the same, just the same
as when I went away. The revolutions tearing
the country asunder were scarcely felt in this

household. My uncle still fully believed that the Confederate cause would be triumphant, and planted his cotton fields and counted his small store of gold, confident that he would add to it at the end of the year.

After the excitement of talking over my adventures while away, had passed, I had time to look more carefully about me, and to detect changes too subtle for superficial observation. Cousin Reuben was making preparations to go away. He had enlisted in a new company just forming, and they expected to enter the regular service some time in March. That he should go about absorbed and grave seemed natural, but my cousin Alicia I could not understand. The serenity of her disposition seemed to have disappeared. One hour she would be unnaturally gay, the next, sunk in deep gloom. She would blush and tremble at the sound of an unexpected footstep, and once I discovered her in tears. She had fallen away until her cheeks were hollow, and she seemed plainer than ever. I fancied she looked taller, too, and drooped

more as she walked. No one seemed to notice
the change in her, and I cautiously questioned
Nell.

" Has Alicia been ill?"

"Ill? no," she said in surprise. "Why do
you ask that?"

"She looks pale and thin."

"She was never fat and blooming."

"She is not—she cannot be in love?"

"Alicia in love! Oh, Rachel, don't let your
imagination run away with you," and Nell
laughed loudly. "Alicia is the least sentimental creature I ever met."

"There you are entirely mistaken," I cried.

"Why, she is a born old maid; you know
she has been one all her life. I see her in the
yard. She is coming in, and I think I must
tell her what you have said."

"Oh, pray don't!" I exclaimed, but she broke
from my detaining hand and ran to the door.

"Alicia, Alicia!"

"What is it, Nell?" pausing at the door.

"Rachel says that you are in love."

"I did not, Alicia. Really, Nell, you are mistaken," I said, in a vexed tone. "I only asked——"

"If I thought so."

Alicia blushed a deep, burning red, and her eyes dropped. Her confusion only threw Nell into fresh laughter, but I divined her secret, and hurriedly said:

"We are teasing you, Alicia. Of course we know that you are not in love."

"I don't mind your nonsense," she said, with a forced smile, and left the room.

For whom could poor Alicia be cherishing a secret passion? It seemed ridiculous to connect her with a romance. We had never known her to have a lover. She held herself aloof from men, and they never seemed attracted to her.

When I came in from my ride late that afternoon I passed through the parlor. Cousin Reuben sat by a table drawn near one of the front windows, with writing materials before him, but his slight figure was huddled up, his

face hidden in his hands. His attitude expressed an abandonment of woe that startled me.
I crossed the room to him, laid my hand on his
shoulder.

"Cousin Reuben, what in the world is the
matter?" I cried, sharply.

He straightened up instantly, brushing his
hair back in confusion.

"Nothing at all. I—I came in here to write
some letters, but my thoughts wouldn't work
very freely, and——"

"They must have been giving you a great
deal of trouble" I interrupted, dryly. "Dear
Cousin Reuben, you are in a desperate strait
about something. I can read it in your face,
your eyes," I continued, softly, half shocked as
he turned unwittingly to the light, and I saw
the lines of suffering on his brow and about his
mouth.

He shifted uneasily in his chair and plucked
at the penwiper with nervous fingers.

"I—I am going away, Rachel."

"Yes."

8

"Perhaps I shall never return. Do you remember young Bledsoe, home on a short furlough last fall?"

"I do."

"He was killed in battle a few weeks ago."

Was it the terror of war upon him?

"Are you—are you *afraid?*" I whispered.

He flushed deeply, and seemed to stiffen in
every muscle.

"Afraid? no; but I don't wonder you think
so, I have hung back so long, when it is the
duty of every man in the country to shoulder
arms. Rachel, it is leaving her that takes
away my strength, my courage, my very heart."

"*Her?*" I echoed, blankly.

"Yes. I loved her almost at first sight, and
to see her day after day for months—well, it
has not cured me."

"Oh, Nell! Nell!" I thought; "how could
you trifle with this kind, faithful heart so cruelly?" "Poor fellow!" I murmured aloud, tenderly.

"Don't pity me, Rachel. She does not love

me; how could she ?" with a slighting, scornful
glance at his own insignificant person, " but I
am glad that I love her. It has been a torment,
but also an intoxicating delight to me. I never
really lived until I met her. It was a revela-
tion to me."

I listened, half amazed to hear the quiet, reserved man talk so. Who would have suspected such passion, such ardent feeling under
that exterior ?

" Is she not beautiful, Rachel ? "

" Yes," I admitted, grudgingly.

" And so sweet and true."

" She is a coquette, Cousin Reub," I cried,
rashly, out of all patience with him.

" A coquette ? oh, no."

" But she is; I know her. She does not mean
any harm, but she can no more help leading a
man on, playing with his feelings, than a cat
can help torturing a mouse. Oh, Cousin Reub,
I am sorry for you; I am sorry for any one who
loves our dear wayward Nell."

He had been walking about the room, but as

I finished speaking he paused and stared at me.

"Nell! who has been talking about Nell?"

"I have."

"What has she to do with this matter?"

Then I concluded that he must be utterly out of his mind to rave about a girl one moment, and be surprised to hear her name the next.

"You said that you were in love with her."

"With Nell? you must be dreaming. Would I give a thought to her by the side of Alicia?"

I sat down, strength leaving me in my astonishment. Could it really be true, or was he merely playing on my credulity? Before my mind flashed the two girls, one radiant, beautiful, the other so pale and plain.

"I thought you said that she was beautiful."

"She is," he exclaimed.

I looked searchingly at him, but found only truth in his eyes. It was an honest delusion. His love had transformed her, or else he recognized a spirit more beautiful than flesh

and blood. Awe fell upon me at the mysterious power of this love, transmuting all things
it touched into purest gold. I thought of Arnold
Lambert and Elinor Sims. So, perhaps, he
loved her, while her heart was given to another man; so I loved him. Cousin Reuben
began mechanically to put his writing materials together. While doing so he turned his
head and glanced out through the window.
His face flushed, his eyes kindled. I softly rose
and looked over his shoulder.

My cousins had driven over to the village
early in the afternoon to pay a visit. They
had just returned, and were stepping from the
carriage. When they entered the gate they
paused for a moment, side by side, to look at
something above or beyond the house, and
never had the contrast between them seemed
so striking. Nell looked fresh and blooming
as a flower, soft curls falling upon her neck
and shoulders, her lips parted in a smile.
Alicia was colorless and wan, her long slender
neck rising above the collar of her mantle, un-

softened by the smallest curled lock, dark
smooth bands of hair just showing under the
brim of her bonnet. Nell tripped up the walk
to the piazza humming "Dixie," but Alicia
lingered to gather a handful of the yellow jon-
quils blooming thickly along the flagged border. The closing light of the mild February
day shone out of the west against her tall thin
figure, the gray strings of her bonnet fluttered
in the wind rising in chilly gusts.

I regarded her with new interest, tried to see
her through Cousin Reuben's eyes, to invest
her with all the graces and fascinating charms
of a woman deeply beloved, but it was only
Alicia, plain Alicia, looking a little chilly and
desolate in the falling dusk. Unconscious of
our regard she strolled along, plucking the
flowers and arranging them, occasionally lifting her eyes in a pensive look to the evening
sky. Cousin Reuben drew a long and quiver-
ing sigh.

"Have you told her?"

"No, I have not had the courage. I dare

not risk defeat yet. I must master my feelings first."

"Do you think you will do it here?"

"No, but I hope to when far away in the army."

"How do you know but she loves you?"

"Don't!" he said huskily. "She is scarcely friendly with me. At first she was frank and kind, kinder than you or Nell, but lately she has avoided me. I understand. She does not wish to give me the pain of a refusal, she——"

"Go this moment and ask her," I said, sure that at last I understood the change in my cousin Alicia.

"But, Rachel——"

"You are blind as a mole, Cousin Reuben, and so is she."

He caught my hand, hope lighting up his face.

"Is there any chance for me?"

"If there is not — but go, and we will finish this talk later."

I stood by the window and watched him as

he went down the walk to her. I fancied that
I could see the color overspreading her face as
he paused at her side. They went away across
the lawn to the garden, and were lost to my
view. I laughed aloud at the thought of those
two going through the world together, so ill
assorted as far as appearances went, even
while tears of sympathy for them in their happiness, blinded my eyes.

Uncle Charles was greatly surprised and
not very well pleased at first with the engagement of his elder daughter, but she looked so
tremulously blooming and happy, blushing
and paling if you but glanced at her, that he
could not withhold his blessing. Then the
question of a speedy marriage was propounded
by Cousin Reuben, and eagerly advocated by
Nell and me. The whole affair struck Nell as
being the most delicious jest, but the excitement of a wedding was irresistible. As usual,
Uncle Charles yielded to the arguments and
entreaties of his family, and the whole household fell zealously to work preparing the

bride's wardrobe. The lovers themselves were of no practical service in these preparations.

Only a few near neighbors were bidden to the marriage, but a great feast was spread, and the slaves were given a holiday and a dance. It was a happy wedding, but we all shed a few tears except the bridegroom, who stared at his tall bride with adoring eyes.

It was at the close of the evening that Uncle Charles came up to me, and whispered, " Is this scene painful to you, Rachel ? "

" Painful ? no," I said, astonished and puzzled.

" You are cured, then—you have entirely forgotten that—that fellow ? "

My cheeks turned scarlet. I thought he had forgotten that confession made to him before I went away in the autumn.

" Yes," I said, deliberately; " I have forgotten him."

" Then I hope you'll soon follow Alicia's example. A woman fulfills her highest duties only when she becomes a wife and mother."

I went up to my room.   The festivities were
all over; I could hear the closing of doors and
windows in the lower part of the house, the
laughing voices of the negroes returning to the
"quarters."   The fitful glow of a bonfire still
shone against my window, and, when I looked
out, I saw a few dusky couples whirling slowly
around the burning heap, dancing a farewell
reel.   At last they stamped out the fire, and
stole away to their cabins.

It would be a long, long time before I should
follow my cousin's example.

CHAPTER XI.

IN three weeks Cousin Reuben was to join his company, but the shadow of separation was not allowed to cloud the first days of the honey-moon. We left them undisturbed to their fleet-ing joy, for they seemed to grudge every mo-ment spent apart. Into those three weeks a lifetime of love and hope was crowded. I have never witnessed such intense happiness, such feeling. They seemed to think of no one in the world but each other. Once, Alicia took me around the waist, and, pressing her head against my shoulder, said:

"I am selfish, Rachel, but I cannot help it. It seems to me that I must make the most of these perfect days with him, that they will never be repeated."

" We know how it is; we do not blame you."

"I doubt if you know. You must love, Rachel, if you would be able to enter into the feelings of others. Love is, of all things, the one to be experienced to be understood."

I stroked her head, while across my mental vision flashed the picture of a mountain campfire, with a Union officer lounging before it.

"Yes, I suppose so," I said, calmly.

"You have not loved yet, Rachel. Oh, I hope I shall be near you when you do. I want to see how you take it; but it will be violently, I know," and she laughed, softly.

I hugged my secret close, trembling lest she should discover it.

"What if Reuben does not come back to me, Rachel?" absorbed in her own hopes and fears again. "Sometimes I feel sure that he will not, that when he goes away I shall never see him on earth again."

"Oh, now you are foolish," I said, cheerfully. "These raw troops will not be put in dangerous places, of course. Cousin Reuben will be perfectly safe, and, I dare say, when we have whipped the Yankees, he will become a great planter with plenty of land and negroes."

" You think so ? I hope your prophecy will come true. It is strange that they should want to interfere with our rights, try to take away our liberties."

" And our property," I added.

" Yes. What is it to them if we have slaves? They are fighting as desperately as if we were barbarians. What would become of the negroes if they were freed ? "

That problem was entirely beyond my grasp. It seemed such a natural and proper thing for the negroes to serve us. They were so much a part of our property that I could not contemplate them in a state of freedom. It was almost as absurd as turning the cattle out, and saying:

" Go hence—set up a kingdom of your own. You no longer belong to me."

" The Northern people are simply mistaken about this matter, Alicia," I said, judicially, " as well as some of our own countrymen who sympathize with them, and it is a mistake that must be whipped out of them. We have right and justice on our side, and the day

will come when they'll be glad to acknowledge it."

It was in her four-and-twentieth year that
Rachel Douglas made that speech. She has
lived to see the foolishness of it.

It was the first day of April that we journeyed
to Atlanta—I to join the Amateurs again, the
others to see Cousin Reuben off. That night
the company was invited to the theatre, and at
the close of the entertainment they all rose and
stood in a body, while the Amateurs sang
" Good-bye " for them.

My voice quavered uncertainly several times,
for I could not help remembering that I had
sung that song to Captain Lambert, and then I
knew that in this audience there were two
hearts nigh to breaking. In the small band of
uniformed men before us stood Cousin Reuben,
his head turned to one side, his eyes fixed on
Alicia, who sat in a remote corner, rigid and
pale, but with hot tears stealing down her face,
and falling in single, glittering drops on her
bosom. She seemed unconscious of her tears,

her eyes answering his rapt gaze in a passion
of love and silent anguish. Her suppressed
emotion affected me far more deeply than the
wildest outburst.

The next morning she parted from her husband composedly, as a brave soldier's wife
should, and returned home with her father and
sister.

The summer passed rather quietly in Atlanta.
I continued my study and practice of music;
singing with the Amateurs having roused a certain ambition in me. We went off on several
little tours, receiving a cordial welcome everywhere. The Ladislaws continued to be the life
and controlling influence of the company, im-
parting their enthusiasm to the lukewarm, and
their courage to the weak. I fell more deeply in
love with them every day, and always regarded
my acquaintance with them as a peculiarly
fortunate thing for me. But Elinor Sims and I
were drawn no nearer together. I could not
overcome my intense dislike of her unwomanly
conduct, nor the contempt with which it in-

spired me, and when she had become fully convinced that I did not care for her friendship
she treated me with as much proud, chilling
indifference as though I had been the wrong-
doer. We were always polite and agreeable to
each other when thrown together, but hastened
to separate as quickly as possible. Once Lieutenant Devreau was reported wounded, and,
amid our noisy expressions of regret, she stood
pale and silent. But I saw the quiver of her
lip, the strained expression of fear in her eyes,
and hardened my heart with the righteous feeling that she deserved to suffer. We hold justice in high esteem when it metes out punish-
ment to our neighbor: it becomes injustice only
when turned against our own shortcomings.

Mary Ladislaw was too much absorbed in the
great events of the war, and the thousand de-
mands on her time and sympathy, to pay much
attention to the misunderstanding between two
young women, but she did once say to me:

"I wish you would be more friendly with
Elinor. She was strongly attracted to you at

first, but you have shown so little desire for her
regard, that I think she is fairly discouraged
in her attempts to know you well."

"What do *you* think of her ?" I asked, point-
edly.

"That she is a strong, as well as lovely,
character," she said, warmly. "You cannot
dislike her, Rachel, and yet to be cold, persis-
tently cold, toward anyone without cause
doesn't seem natural to you."

"It isn't. I hope that I am too just for that."

"Then why can you not get on with her ?"

"I—really, I don't know," I said, stammering and blushing over the equivocation, but for
once generosity alone prompted the reply.
If she had not confided in Mrs. Ladislaw, I did
not intend to be the one to give her the repu-
tation of a coquette. Mary should be kept in
ignorance, if it depended on me to betray
Elinor.

"I think that I must tell you her family history some time," she said; "then you will understand her better."

9

I felt no curiosity to know it; I understood
her well enough, I thought, and secretly determined to discourage all confidences about
her.

"Certainly, if you wish," I said, none too
graciously, and the subject was dropped for that
time.

It was the first of September that Mr. Ladislaw received a telegram, stating that his brother
was dangerously wounded and lying in a camp-
hospital near Chattanooga. The despatch had
been delayed, and Mr. Ladislaw left at once,
fearful that he should not find his brother alive.
The day after her husband's departure, Mary
was seized with a great desire to follow him,
and asked me to go with her.

"You are strong and fearless, Rachel, and
disposed to like danger and adventure. I would
also ask Elinor, but her grandfather is ill, and
her mother cannot spare her."

"*I* will go with you," I cried, eagerly. "I
would not miss the opportunity for—for the
world, hardly."

" Must you write to your uncle ? "

" Oh, no ! " I said, recklessly, so excited and charmed with the prospect of the trip, and the thought of approaching the armies, that I would not stop to think of Uncle Charles, and my duty to him as my guardian.

" I don't believe that we ought to take your servants."

" I will send them home."

" But can you get on without them ? "

" Oh, certainly," I replied, with as much promptitude as though I had been in the habit of waiting on myself, whereas I had never really been a day without a servant in my life.

When I informed old Ned and Milly that I intended to send them home, they were perfectly aghast.

" Ain't you comin' too, Miss Rachel ? " cried my old nurse.

And then I could no longer conceal my delight, but told them where I expected to go; imagination playing such tricks with my tongue that I wound up by declaring that I intended

to be in one battle at least, before I returned.
They listened in horror, and, when I had finished, burst into lamentations and entreaties to
be permitted to remain with me. I firmly refused, even when Aunt Milly fell at my feet, and
grasped my skirts in her shaking hands, with
piteous sobs and cries.

Tears streamed down my face.

"Hush! hush! or people will think I am
beating you," I said, heartily repenting that
lurid account of the manifold dangers I expected to encounter.

Ned grew suddenly calm.

"Git up from dar, Milly, an' quit pesterin'
Miss Rachel. When you gwine to leave us,
honey?" wiping his eyes on his coat-sleeve.

"To-morrow," I said, giving him an approv-
ing smile for his obedience. "I shall leave all
my things here, but you and Aunt Milly can
take what you please home with you."

"Yes'm," meekly; then he took Aunt Milly
by the arm and led her away into the next
room. Presently they both came back, com-

posed, almost cheerful, and I could but think
on the transitory nature of their emotion. Old
Ned made various respectful inquiries about
my journey, and received the pass I gave him
with an humble expression of gratitude. They
were to leave for Decatur about the same time
that I did for Chattanooga, and I gave them a
liberal supply of money for the trip, knowing
that the pass would enable them to go alone.
I also entrusted to them long letters to Uncle
Charles and my cousins.

In the afternoon Mrs. Ladislaw asked me to
go with her to see Elinor. I consented, without much reluctance, feeling so complacent
over my good fortune that I was quite pleased
to say good-bye to the whole city. I had never
been in Elinor's home before, and glanced
about with some curiosity when we were shown
into the parlor. It was evident that they were
people of wealth, as well as taste and refine-
ment, simplicity and elegance were so happily
combined in the decoration of the room.

Mrs. Sims came in with her daughter, but

she looked like a weak and indolent woman, and I turned from her faded prettiness to look at the pictures on the walls. Some of them were portraits, and I could not repress a slight exclamation when my eyes fell on one hanging above the mantel. It was Arnold Lambert.

"What did you say, Miss Douglas?" Mrs. Sims inquired, in her languid drawl.

I blushed scarlet, and, looking at Elinor, saw that her cheeks had reddened also. Her eyes had followed mine to that picture.

" I should like to take Rachel out to—to the grape-arbor, mother," she said, hastily rising.

" Certainly, my love; but I think it would be pleasanter to order some grapes brought in."

Nearly a year had passed since those chance meetings with Captain Lambert; but the sight of his portrait roused such emotion in me that I was glad to follow Elinor silently from the room. We walked about the garden, gathered a few roses, and she told me that they owned a place near Decatur.

"The old Montgomery place?" I asked, quickly.

"Yes; do you know it?"

"It is near my uncle's," I said, understanding at last why Arnold Lambert lingered in the deserted garden and around the old house. It was for her sake.

We returned to the house, and on the back piazza encountered a tall, handsome, feeble-looking old man, walking slowly, half-supported by a stout negro. He stopped to speak to us, and I felt my heart go out to him, such benignity beamed from his eyes, melted the stern lines of his mouth. A beautiful, fascinating smile overspread his noble face, and I lingered at his side a few minutes, talking with him. It was Judge Lenoir, Elinor's grandfather.

"He looks as I imagine Goethe must have looked in his old age," I said, when we left him.

She looked at me in surprise.

"Do you read Goethe?"

"I have read more about him than of his own

works. *Wilhelm Meister*, *The Confessions of a Fair Saint* and *Faust* I have read. My uncle has a very good library, and I have always had free access to it."

My knowledge of those books seemed to impress her.

" You are a remarkable girl, Rachel. I admire your spirit and your gifts. I wish that we could be friends."

"So do I," I replied, touched again by her frankness, and flattered by her admiration.

But we had no time for further speech. Mrs. Ladislaw called me, and we left rather hastily, as there were still some arrangements to make for our journey. The next day we left Atlanta on the northbound train for Chattanooga, and the stirring scenes of war.

CHAPTER XII.

WE did not enter Chattanooga at all, for the Confederates were already preparing to leave the place—finding it necessary to sacrifice that vantage-ground in order to protect Atlanta. We stopped at a small station near the town, and the first person I saw when I stepped from the train to the platform was—old Ned, dressed in his best clothes, and with a lean, rusty-looking carpet-bag in his hand! His expression was a mingling of defiance and fright, and the thought crossed my mind that perhaps he was deserting me for the enemy. Surprise and indignation held me speechless for a moment, and I turned my back on him. Then I heard a soft, insinuating little cough at my elbow, and there he stood, hat in hand, staring humbly at the floor.

" What are you doing here, Ned?" I inquired in my sternest tone.

" I couldn't he'p comin', 'deed I couldn't."

" I see, you thought it a good opportunity to
run away. You might have told me that you
wanted to go to the Yankees."

" Now, Miss Rachel, honey, what you want
ter talk to me dat way for? I ain't no mo'
gwine to de Yankees dan you is. I ain't one
o' dem dat deserts a post o' duty."

" You have certainly disobeyed me."

" So I has; but did you t'ink, honey, dat
I'd let you come 'way up here by you'se'f? You
kin beat me, Miss Rachel, but I ain't gwine to
be driv' home, 'tel you go."

Tears were trickling down his wrinkled face,
but he looked very obstinate, for all that. My
face relaxed.

" Forgive him, Rachel," Mrs. Ladislaw whispered.

" Where is Aunt Milly?" I inquired.

" She done gone home. Dat 'oman is sich
er fool she won't mine a word I say 'dout a

beatin'. Is dem t'ings yourn, Miss Rachel?" he asked in a cheerful tone, and eagerly loaded himself with our wraps and bags.

In the exciting days following, we were very glad that he had been disobedient enough to follow me, and I often longed for the motherly care of my old nurse.

We learned that the hospital had been moved the day before to a safe point not far from Chickamauga Creek, and it would be necessary to hire a conveyance to take us across the country to it. It was then Mrs. Ladislaw began to realize the seriousness of her attempt to follow her husband. She turned to me.

"Shall we go on, Rachel?"

"By all means," I said, firmly.

The fool may appear brave because he lacks understanding. The true hero is the man who combines courage and discretion. It is the same with a heroine. My courage was the bravery of a fool.

"We can return to Atlanta to-night," she continued, hesitatingly.

"And we can go on to the camp to-night," I replied.

"That is true, and it would be cowardly in us to run away from the prospect of a few hardships, when our dear boys are fighting and dying for us. Come, we will carry out our first plan."

For a hundred dollars in Confederate money, a farmer, living near the station, agreed to drive us over to the hospital. We were dismayed when he brought his team around, for it was a rough cart with some splint chairs placed in it for us to sit on, and a yoke of oxen to draw it. It was already approaching nightfall, and with such a conveyance we would probably be several hours on the road.

"De springs air done wore out o' dis wagon, Miss Rachel," Uncle Ned said to me after an examination.

"There never wus enny at fust," said our driver, with a humorous grin. "Git in, ladies; these creeturs kin travel faster'n you think for. Hi, thar, you nigger! he'p yer missus inter the waggin."

The roads were in a fearful state, cut into deep ruts, the wagon wheels sinking almost to the hub in the soft, heavy mud. We were bumped and jolted until we were bruised and sore all over, and fell into grim silence. Uncle Ned alone remained cheerful and talkative, engaging the driver in a discussion of the condition of the country, and airing his knowledge of the various cities he had visited. The countryman listened to him rather scornfully, evidently irritated by the old man's superior knowledge and his contentment in a condition of servitude. He did not speak his mind very plainly, but he said enough for us to understand that he sympathized with the Union. Mary's animation returned, her eyes flashed, her cheeks grew pink. " Do you mean to say that you are willing to have your rights all taken from you ?"

" They ain't tuk nothin' from me, an' hit 'ud be a plagued sight better tu let the niggers go free th'n ter spill so much good white blood a-fightin' ter keep em in slavery," he said, doggedly.

She tried to make him understand that we
were fighting for the sake of principle, for the
defense of our homes, our liberty. "An'
theyer fightin' for principle an' liberty too.
Hit's hard tu onderstan' how both sides kin be
a-fightin' fer the same thing an' agin one er-
nuther. Gee thar, Ab'slum. I'm fer the old
flag, mum. Hit's the one what Washington an'
all them other Revolutioneries fit an' died fer,
an' I reckon hit's better'n enny new un we uns
could git up."

"Perhaps you intend to deliver us over to the
enemy?" said Mary with fine scorn in her eyes.

He turned and looked at her, and stroked the
ragged beard on his chin.

"Law, now, do yer think that o' me? I
don't know ez the Yankees 'ud want sech prisoners," eying us reflectively. "Wimmin kin
use their tongues like ole Haley when they git
mad, an' fight an' scratch between theyselves,
but as soldiers or prisoners o' war, I don't think
they er o' much o' count."

We rushed into an ardent defense of women,

and drew on history for examples of female courage, but he merely smiled skeptically and stroked his beard.

Night came on, and I was forcibly reminded of our journey from North Carolina by the rough and hilly country through which we passed. It seemed to me those oxen traveled with incredible slowness, or else we were impatient to reach the end of our journey. We met several parties of scouting Confederates who politely saluted us, staring curiously at us the while. The stars came out brilliantly in the frosty atmosphere, but we had no moon to light the way. I grew faint with hunger, and Mary opened a small flask of liquor, and made me drink a little of it, but that only turned me giddy and light-headed without appeasing my stomach.

It had such a peculiar effect on me that I fancied sparks of fire were flashing from my eyes, and I laughed hysterically at everything that was said.

It was about 9 o'clock in the night that we

halted at a cross-roads, and the countryman
left his team long enough to examine a sign-
board. He came back and calmly announced
that we were on the wrong road.

"I missed it at Turner's crossin'," he said.

"What are we to do, then?" cried my friend
in despair.

"We uns kin turn back, or go through the
settlement road."

"What shall we decide on, Rachel?" said
Mary, in an appealing tone.

My head still felt empty and light as a feather,
and it required an effort to suppress a foolish
giggle, as I said:

"The settlement road, if he knows the way
and it is nearer."

What a journey that was! I have only a
confused recollection of its length and duration,
but I know that Mary and I resigned ourselves
to the worst that could come before it ended.
Uncle Ned crouched in the bottom of the
wagon, and clung to our chairs, muttering alternate prayers and maledictions.

"This is a remarkable experience, Rachel," my friend whispered.

"I only hope we shall live through it," I replied.

We turned the brow of a hill, descended it at a rapid pace, and the next we knew, team and wagon were stuck fast in a bog. A new road had been cut around it, but in the darkness our driver missed that. It was pitch-dark in the swamp, and the imaginary dangers of the situation were far more frightful than the real ones. The farmer lighted a torch from some pine he had stowed away in the wagon—I wonder it had not occurred to him to do it before—and we looked shudderingly around on the wild scene. We were evidently near a stream, and the morass was caused by the overflow. Black pools of water with clumps of grass, rank flags and "cat-tails" growing out of them reflected the light glassily, and sweet-gum and poplar trees bent thick interlacing branches overhead. The poor oxen were sunk to their knees in the treacherous black bog, and the wagon was steadily settling.

10

The driver and Uncle Ned leaped out, and waded to firmer ground to find brush and decayed timber to throw into the bog for us to step on, when we left the wagon.   I held the torch, meanwhile, the hot pitch dripping down on my hands, and the sooty smoke turning my face to the dusky tint of an African's.   Mary descended to the rude bridge first, and then I followed after, throwing the blazing pine out on dry ground, but scarcely had I touched the ground when a great frog leaped across my foot.   I loathe frogs.   The mere sight of one turns me faint with terror, and when that creature's shiny head and long legs flashed across my vision, I screamed and ran back through the marsh until I reached the opposite bank, with my shoes and stockings in a pitiable state, and my skirts splashed to the knee.

The oxen were unyoked and driven out, and after repeated efforts on the part of the men to move the wagon we were about to abandon it, when a squad of soldiers, returning from a foraging expedition, came to our relief. Never had

the sight of a gray uniform been more welcome
to me. Our sad plight called forth their sympathy, as well as afforded them a good deal of
merriment. They jeered at the countryman,
even while they pulled his wagon out of the
mud, and proposed to see us safely to the hospital, an offer he declined.

"No; I started with 'em, an' I'm agoin' to
take 'em tu the end o' thar journey, but I'll be
dad-blamed if onnuther woman ever gits me tu
haul her ennywhar; no, not for er thousand
dollars o' Confederate money."

The soldiers gallantly escorted us the remainder of the way, but we were glad almost
to weeping when the white tents of the camp-
hospital rose in ghostly array on our vision.
Subdued activity reigned. In a remote part of
the camp new tents were being stretched, and
guards paced slowly and wearily on their beats,
while those who had been relieved lay rolled
in their blankets on the naked ground, asleep.

The soldiers who had befriended us carried
the news of our arrival through the camp, and

presently Mr. Ladislaw came out of a tent and
swiftly toward us. He looked worn and sad,
but never nobler and handsomer than at that
moment. His eyes lighted up as they fell on
his wife; the lines of his face relaxed.

"Mary! you here?" he exclaimed. "I could
not believe it when they told me."

She ran to him.

"Oh, Henry, how glad I am to be with you
again!" Then she threw her arms about his
neck and burst into tears, the first I had ever
seen her shed for herself.

CHAPTER XIII.

THAT night we ate soldiers' rations, and slept in a soldier's tent, and rose in the morning refreshed and ready for duty, though rather stiff and sore from the experiences of the evening before. Edward Ladislaw had received his wound at the battle of Bridgeport, Alabama, and there was but slight hope of his recovery. Mary took her place by his bunk. He was a young fellow, her husband's only brother, and loved by her very tenderly. Her husband opposed our remaining in the hospital.

" It is no place for delicate women," he said, when arguing the matter with us.

" Delicate women often have stronger nerves than the bravest men, my darling," said Mary. " I know now that it was wrong to ask Rachel to come with me, but——"

"Rachel does not repent coming!" I exclaimed. "Nurses are needed, I am sure, and I have witnessed suffering enough in the Atlanta hospitals to realize some of the sights we'd have to look on here. If the women of a country cannot fight its battles, they can bind up the wounds of those who do."

"Good for you, Rachel Douglas!" cried my friend applaudingly, and Mr. Ladislaw permitted us to have our way.

We lodged in a farm-house within a stone's throw of the camp, a mere cabin with a loft. We slept in the loft, climbing up to it on a movable ladder. The bed, stuffed with sweet-smelling straw and grasses, was most comfortable to us, though its sheets were homespun and scanty. The roof sloped down very low, and great fat spiders spun their webs in the corners and over the surface of the boards. The family numbered four, a man, his wife and two daughters. The girls were slender, hardy-looking creatures, dipped a great deal of snuff, and went barefooted. They belonged to that

peculiar class of Georgians called " crackers "
now, but they were known in those days as
" poor white trash." They had no ardent
political feelings or patriotism. They had
nothing to lose, perhaps nothing to gain by the
war, and looked on it with indifference, even
when its tumult swept around them. The
common love of humanity caused them to
minister to the sick and wounded solders, but
beyond that they seemed to feel no interest in
the issue of the struggle.

Uncle Ned was secretly very unhappy. Between his fears for me and the discomforts of
his own life, he went about with a very gloomy
face. He presaged the most grievous misfortunes, and implored me to return home, but
I had only to remind him that it was through
his own disobedience he suffered, to send him
from my presence in humble silence. His
faithful, dog-like devotion to me never relaxed
through all the days of hardship and peril,
and some of them were exceedingly dark.

I will not linger over those experiences as

a hospital nurse, nor attempt to describe any
of the movements of the two armies. They
belong to history, and the details of every
skirmish have been told and retold. It was
the beginning of that campaign which was
to end in Sherman's march to the sea, though
little did we think then that Georgia was to be
laid waste by siege and battle from the mountains to the Atlantic border.

Subdued but intense excitement prevailed.
The armies were changing their position every
day, skirmishing and manœuvring for ad-
vantages, and to the hospital fresh cases were
constantly brought.

The excitement, the misery, were in strange
contrast to the tranquil autumn days on which
the sun rose and set in unclouded splendor.
One could scarcely believe that the smoke
hanging over the hills and softening the sun-
sets to dull red came from the fusillade of
arms, or that the crowded heaps of freshly
turned earth in a sedge-field were the graves
of dead soldiers, borne daily from the camp-

hospital. Yet death became a familiar presence
to all. The terror and the awe of it vanished.
Men jested about it, even when its grisly hand
lay on them, and yielded to it as to the loving
grasp of a friend, and we women were hardened
to tearlessness in its presence.

In a day or two after Mary and I arrived at
the hospital, two maiden ladies—sisters—came
from their home, near Cartersville, to join in
the work of nursing. They had not a great
deal of experience or nerve, but enthusiasm
and a heroic desire to sacrifice themselves carried them through the most sickening and trying scenes. They entered into the work with
the holy fervor and zeal of religious devotees;
and I know that, simple, plain and middle-aged
as they were, they were regarded as saints by
the poor fellows under their ministrations. It
was not only a glorious duty they performed,
but the experience colored their monotonous
lives with romance. To be held in such rever-
ential esteem and affection suffused existence
with light and joy. Their name was Mande-

ville—Sarah Ann and Jane—and they could trace their ancestry back to remote English origin. Miss Jane was my favorite, being softer and gentler than her sister, and we had frequent walks together through the autumn woods when we wished to escape from the discord of pain and death. I could trace a likeness between her and my cousin Alicia—a faded likeness, for her dark hair had turned gray, and her tall, slight figure stooped, not from habit, but encroaching age. She was a woman of fine perceptions and sensitive feelings. She had an artistic eye for colors, and I have seen her face light up with pleasure over the grouping of autumn leaves. Her life had been passed principally on a plantation, but one visit to the great cities of the North had enlightened her mind as to the possibilities of life beyond the environments of the planter's home. Her allegiance to the Confederacy caused her to speak of that journey with reserve. To her simple mind it appeared disloyal to mention the enemy's country, and a delicate air of self-deprecation marked all she said about it.

I saw less of Mary during those days than of Miss Jane, for she spent most of the time at the bedside of Edward Ladislaw, using all her woman's tenderness and skill in nursing, to save his life. But it was without avail. Her face, worn with watching, saddened as the days passed.

"I fear that it is only a question of time, Rachel," she said. "But I am glad we came. Henry needs me."

"It is only a question of time with all of us, and I sometimes wonder whether a few months or years can make any material difference," I replied, heavy - heartedly, oppressed by the tragical side of life.

One afternoon she came out to the cabin to me. I leaned over the gate, looking away into the valley withdrawn from the declining light of the sun, and wondering what new developments the morrow would bring forth in the situation of the armies. I was instantly struck with a subtle change in my friend's face, and went out to meet her. The touch of my hand on her shoulder unlocked the reservoir of emotion. Her lip trembled, tears overflowed her weary eyes.

"Is he worse, Mary?"

"He is gone, Rachel—gone."

"Dead!" I exclaimed; then was silent, shocked in spite of myself.

"Yes. Poor Henry! he takes it hard."

Her thought was more for her husband than for the young soldier who had passed beyond her care.

"What will you do?"

"He must be buried here for the present. Henry thinks it best. The country is so torn up it would be wellnigh impossible to take him to Atlanta, now."

That evening we stood around the new-made grave and saw Edward Ladislaw's body lowered into it, clothed in the faded gray uniform he had worn through the service, and wrapped in a military cloak. The light of a pale new moon hanging remotely in the western sky, silvered the waving sedge in the field, while all the country beyond lay in mysterious shadow. That spectral radiance touched the uncovered heads of the mourners, the brother and sister and two or three old soldiers who had hobbled out from the camp to pay the last honors to their favorite officer. Miss Sarah Ann Mandeville read the burial service, or rather repeated it with the book open before her, and then the earth was thrown in again by Uncle Ned, a rough boulder marking the head of the grave. It was not the only burial I attended while there, but it was one of the saddest.

Miss Jane and I watched with the wounded until midnight that night; then she shared the couch in the cabin loft with me. Daylight was shining through the north end window, a square hole with a wooden shutter, and through the chinks in the walls, when I awoke next morning. A sense of weariness from the vigil of the night still oppressed me, in spite of my youth and good health, and I lay in that listless state in which the mind works clearly, but the body is inert, when a deep boom apparently shook the solid earth beneath us, and reverberated in a thousand broken echoes.

"What is it?" I cried aloud, shaken with sudden terror.

"The firing of cannon," said my companion in an awe-struck tone. Her delicate withered face blanched. She sat up in bed and listened, and the strings of her muslin nightcap vibrated softly with the fluttering pulse in her lean white throat. Another explosion came, heavier than the first. We got out of bed and crept to the window, and pushed open the shutter. Sunlight streamed across the broken hilly country in slanting golden beams from the east, and rosy clouds hung about the top of Lookout Mountain, or skimmed away across the sky. A flock of buzzards sailed round and round in the upper sky, their broad black wings casting fleeting shadows on the distant landscape. The course of Chickamauga Creek was clearly traced by a line of white mist rising and spread-

ing into thin vapor as the sunlight touched it.
A glistening freshness marked the incoming
day, and the still air was bitten with the
keenness of frost.   So fine seemed the beauty
and repose of the world in that first glimpse, it
was like a new creation; but strange sounds
vibrated on our hearing, and presently the
awful roar of cannon rent that semblance of
peace asunder.

It was the beginning of the great battle of
Chickamauga.

The recollections of that day are tinged
through and through with the lurid hue of
blood.   Of its experiences I cannot write.
Once, overcome with the horror of it all, and
longing to get away from the sounds of the
guns, I fled to the loft, and buried my head in
the bedclothes.

"Dat you, Miss Rachel, honey?" muttered
a husky voice. I looked up, and saw old Ned
creeping out of a dusty corner, his black face
gray with fear, the whites of his eyes rolling
like marbles.

" What are you doing up here ? " I demanded
severely.

" Honey, I'se dat skeered, it's made me sick
at de stummick, an' my knees is weaker dan
water."

" You are a coward, Uncle Ned," I cried
scornfully.

" I'd ruther be a coward dan have my head
blowed off'n me," he groaned. " Listen at
dat ! " clutching at his trembling legs, as the
cabin shook from the terrific firing. " Dey er
comin' dis way, Miss Rachel; oh ! oh ! may de
Lawd save us from destruction ! "

I pitied but could not reassure him, my own
mind was in such a turmoil. Every moment I
expected to be engulfed and swept away in the
terrible conflict. Smoke darkened the atmosphere until the sun shone through it like a dull
red flame; the fumes of burning powder hung
heavy in the air. From that day war assumed a new and awful significance to me. It was
no longer for the exhibition of chivalry, of
romantic deeds of valor, but for the savage

slaughter of men, the gratification of unbridled hatred.

The wounded and dying were brought in by scores. The rebels were winning the victory, and more than one died with fierce, exultant words on his lips, and the light of passion in his eyes, the bloody passion of war.

In the afternoon Mr. Ladislaw sent Mary and me away from the hospital. "Go, now, and rest. This is no place for you," he said, as new ambulances came in, loaded with mangled, writhing humanity. "Perhaps you can return to-night."

We went away to our refuge, the loft, and tried to talk hopefully, to rouse some sensation of pleasure in the victory of our army, but heavy silence fell upon us. We could think only of the lives lost.

I fell asleep sitting by the window, and it was dusk when consciousness returned. A shawl had been folded about my shoulders, and Uncle Ned crouched patiently on the floor near me. A silence that seemed frightful, after such hideous uproar, brooded over the world.

11

"Mary!" I cried, trembling with fear.

"She done gone back to camp," said old Ned gently.

"Why is everything so still? Are they all dead?" I asked.

"Lawd, honey! it's to be hoped not, but de fightin' has stopped. I been down cookin' you some supper, Miss Rachel. 'Tain't nuffin' but co'n bread and a slice o' bacon, but it'll be streng'henin'."

"I couldn't eat," I sighed wearily.

"Now you try, honey, you try. Starvin' is mighty poor pay."

He coaxed and urged until I went down and ate a part of his rations. I learned from him that the family, overcome with fear, had hastily gathered together a few of their things, and refugeed toward the farther south. The food refreshed me, and we left the deserted cabin and went down to the hospital. I paused on the outer edge of the camp-ground, daunted by the groans wrung from the wounded soldiers they were still bringing in from the battle-field.

The tents had overflowed, and men were lying thickly on the ground.

"Water! water!" was the imploring cry rising from a thousand parched and fevered throats. Here and there a blue-coat lay side by side with the grey, and I saw two poor fellows, enemies on the battle-field, dividing food and drink with one another.

An ambulance drove up near me, and stopped. An officer came forward to inspect the wounded men in it.

"I thought you had orders not to pick up any more Federals?" he said sharply to the driver.

"But he didn't seem to be badly wounded."

"Put him out; he is nearly dead from loss of blood. We must save our own men first."

I pressed forward, as the apparently lifeless body of a Federal officer was placed upon the ground. A thrill of recognition went through me like a shock. I fell on my knees at his side, and turned his face to the light, reading in its set and ghastly features the destiny bringing me to that spot. It was to see Arnold Lambert die.

CHAPTER XIV.

"Don't leave him here!" I pleaded, when my confused senses permitted me to speak.

"Madam—Miss, he is dead," said the officer, calmly.

"He is not dead!" I cried, feeling the faint throb of his heart under my hand. "Oh, it is inhuman not to try to save this life because it belongs to an enemy!"

The man hardened, feeling my speech unjust.

"Do you think we are mean enough to strike an already fallen foe?" he demanded hotly. "It is impossible to care for our own wounded as they should be cared for. Shall this man's life be held in preference to theirs? If you had to make choice between saving a friend or a foe, would you hesitate over it? Not much."

I recognized the justness of his argument, even while blindly angry at his callous indif-

ference to Arnold's fate. I stared down at the
wounded man, sick with grief when I saw blood-
stains on his breast and around the jagged
edges of a bullet-hole in the shoulder of his
coat. Wherever my hand came in contact
with his clothing, that hideous moisture clung
to it.

Nobody had time, it seemed, to waste a
moment's pity on him. When I looked up
Uncle Ned and I were alone with him. The
old man seemed to partially comprehend my
emotion.

"I knowed him, honey, de minnit my
eyes seed him," he whispered. "He stood by
you an' Miss Nell in de mountains; we'll stand
by him here." He bent over to examine the
prostrate man. "He breathes, Miss Rachel."

"We must get him to the cabin," I said
faintly; "he cannot die here." I felt calm but
strained in every nerve. Every fluttering
breath he drew caused me to hold mine with
fear, lest it should be his last. We tried to
lift him, but his weight seemed the weight of

death. Miss Jane Mandeville came near to give water to a wounded soldier, and I called softly to her.

" Come, help me," I entreated.

She came instantly.

" What is it ?"

" A wounded soldier; oh, help us carry him to the house ! "

" A Federal ? "

" A man, a brother, as much as those over there," with a quick gesture toward a group of Confederates. " Don't parley about the color of his clothes."

" Do you know him ? "

" Yes."

She stooped and peered into my face.

I gave my eyes to her scrutiny, and I think she understood my secret. Heaven knows I did not care. I could have proclaimed it to all the world to save his life. Silently she lent her aid, and we carried him to the cabin, and laid him on the bed in the back shed-room.

She remained with me until Uncle Ned had

cut away the clothing from the wounded man's
shoulder, and washed the blood from his lac-
erated flesh. Then, with the experience gathered in the hospital, she pronounced the wound
fairly a slight one.

"Exhaustion and loss of blood have reduced
him to this low ebb, Rachel," she said, and I
could have embraced her in my joy. I felt life
flowing back to my heart, tingling through my
veins. My face must have glowed, for a tinge
of sympathetic color stole into her withered
cheeks, and when I silently pressed her arm
she leaned it against me for a moment. No
nearer did we ever come to confidences about
the matter.

"Your man will attend to him, and be an
excellent nurse, I know. I must go back now
to the poor fellows at the camp. Your—your
friend may have fever for a few days, but I am
sure that he is not fatally wounded."

She went away, and I sat down near the bedside. Uncle Ned had found some tallow
candles, and he had placed one, lighted, on

the table. Its flickering glow fell on Arnold's
face, and I watched every slight change passing over it, in breathless suspense. Would he
presently wake out of that unconscious state,
and recognize me? One hand hung helplessly
down over the edge of the narrow bed. I
raised it gently and laid it on the coverlid, the
color running over my face, even though he
was ignorant of the touch.

A tenderness such as I had never felt before
pulsed through me. It was protective, ma-
ternal, in its depth and intensity; it was a
baptism of new life to my soul. And it all
came through seeing him lying there pale,
helpless, at my mercy. Signs of reviving animation appeared in him, his lips moved,
and bending above him I heard that cry
for—"Water, water," ever on the lips of the
wounded.

I gave him to drink, and he sank back into
that deathlike stillness again. For a week he
alternated between delirium and stupor, recog-
nizing no one. Uncle Ned nursed him with

devotion, and I came and went in a fever of
unrest, my thoughts bound to the narrow limits
of that poor shed, and the struggle for life
going on within it.

Active hostilities between the armies had
ceased for a few days. The Federals, defeated
at Chickamauga, had retreated again to Chattanooga, and our armies were planting their
guns on Missionary Ridge and Lookout Mountain, exultant and confident of other successes.
I heard the news with indifference; loyalty, love
of country, swallowed up in love of Arnold
Lambert.

The cabin was not invaded by our soldiers.
It was tacitly understood that it was to be left
to the nurses, so the presence of the Union
officer remained unknown, except to a few.
The Ladislaws frankly and strongly disapproved
of my charitable conduct toward the stranger,
for I did not betray any former acquaintance
with him.

When Mary stepped to the shed-room door,
and looked on his face for the first time, she

started back, her face hardening as I had never seen it harden before.

"Arnold Lambert, of all men! He is not worthy of your care, Rachel."

I was hurt and indignant.

"I didn't know that you carried your loyalty to such extreme limits," I said, stiffly.

"You know why I dislike this man."

"Yes," I said, thinking that it was because he had loved Elinor Sims; "but I don't see why that should be regarded as a crime. A man has the right to do as he pleases in such matters."

"I differ with you. Duty should——"

"It is not a question of duty," I interrupted, impatiently.

"You talk flippantly, Rachel. An honest foe I respect; a traitor I despise,"and she hastily withdrew, leaving me rather bewildered by her bitter speech.

It is singular how close the truth can come to us without revealing itself. Had I asked one question, shown one doubt that I did not fully understand her, an explanation would have been made, but I was so sure I did understand, that the opportunity profited nothing. Women have less tolerance than men when their prejudices are put to the test. Mary Ladislaw and I held somewhat aloof from each other after that conversation.

"Rachel has the right to her own opinion, Mary," said her husband, gently. "There are few such ardent rebels as we, or so true to the cause."

My implied faithlessness was accepted in silence. Miss Jane Mandeville was my true friend during that strange experience, and a more delicate and tactful soul I never met.

One day I came up from the hospital, and stepped softly across the outer room to the shed. Arnold lay with his face to the wall, and my heart was smitten with fresh pain as I noted the thinness of his cheek and throat.

"How is he now, Uncle Ned?" I asked, in a low tone.

"Hu-sh, Miss Rachel, he done wake up, an' know ever' t'ing," whispered the old man radiantly, as he passed out at the door to bring a fresh bucket of water from the spring.

The invalid turned his head, and looked at me, but it was no longer a wandering gaze. Glad recognition brightened it, and his wan face was suffused with a tinge of color.

"Rachel, come here," he said, faintly.

I went to the bedside, but tenderness, bashful tenderness, held me silent. He stretched out his weak hand, clasped my wrist, then my arm, trying to draw me down to him. In the confusion of the moment I couldn't question his right to do it, but knelt on the floor at the bedside. Quick blushes ran over my face; I gazed at the coverlid rather than at him. "You have been in my thoughts all the time, and when he told me how you saved my life——"

"Who told you?" I asked.

"The old negro, your servant. Rachel, Rachel! it seems too good to be true that you are here with me; that I can speak to you; once more look on your dear, lovely face! Do you remember the rose?"

"You must not talk," I faltered; "it will excite you, bring back the fever."

"Kiss me, then, and I will be silent."

I looked into his entreating eyes for a moment. "Yes, I love you with all my heart," he said so earnestly, with such passion running through his weak tones, I could not doubt it. He raised his arm to my neck, and then I leaned forward, and laid my lips, fresh, red, and tremulous, on his pale mouth. "Dearest!" he whispered, and tried to press me closer to him, but fell back, a groan of pain wrung from him by his wounded shoulder. "Don't leave me, Rachel," as I rose to my feet again.

"I must—you need rest."

"Then come again, come quickly," clinging to my hand.

"Yes, yes," I said, and hastily left the room as Uncle Ned entered it. I went out into the woods and walked, to avoid all companionship. No romance I had ever read, in prose or verse, had prepared me for the reality. A thousand conflicting thoughts whirled through my mind;

shame and joy alternately possessed me. I had
not uttered a tender word to him, yet I had
permitted him to look into my heart and see
that I loved him. It was not until later that I
could think of Elinor Sims, and question my
right to his love. He was still pledged to her,
I did not doubt, and ignorant of her faithlessness.

When I had gone so far in my thoughts,
then I went farther, and doubted if he loved
me at all. His words were merely an impulse
of gratitude. In his weakness the sight of a
familiar face had excited him to say more than
he meant.

I did not see him again until the next evening, and then it was in the presence of Miss
Jane Mandeville. Uncle Ned lay on the floor
asleep, and we stepped softly, and talked in
whispers, not to wake the poor old fellow.
Captain Lambert talked with Miss Jane, but
looked at me, and I felt conscience-smitten under his keenly reproachful gaze. He was
stronger, and declared that he hoped to be

well in a few days. As we were going away,
he called me :

" Miss Douglas, may I trouble you to tight-
en the bandage on my shoulder ? "

I went back to the bedside, and bent over
him. He seized my hand, and pressed it to
his cheek and lips.

" Why have you not been to see me ? I
have expected you, looked for you, every hour
of the day."

" I have been at the hospital. Has Uncle
Ned been careless ? "

" No, no; but I wanted you, Rachel."

" Please let me arrange the bandage," I
said, as coolly as I could, but trembling like a
leaf, " for Miss Jane is waiting for me."

" It is all right; but go, if you are so anxious
to be rid of me. I know you have the right to
neglect me, that I am at your mercy, but yesterday——"

" We were both hasty," I said falteringly.

His eyes looked steadily at me, compelled
mine to meet them.

" Do you repent ? "

I could not say yes; I did not want to say no.

" Do you repent, Rachel ? " his voice rising, a feverish flush appearing in his thin face. " She tortures me with a coquette's tricks," he muttered to himself with a sigh, and released my hand.

The unjust suspicion stung me into speech:

" I do not : how can you think so ? "

" Because you are so capricious—tender yesterday, hard and cold to-day. Am I so much a stranger to you that you feel afraid of me ? I have had no chance to woo you, dearest, or make you love me. I know it, but it has not been my own fault. I wanted to speak when we were together in that garden, but feared to risk my chances. Think of the uncertainty, the perils of war, of my helplessness, and be frank with me."

Miss Jane coughed in the outer room, and I heard her walking lightly over the floor. It was to remind me that she was waiting. I stooped lower over the bed; my arm encircled

his head for an instant. " I am taking everything into consideration," I whispered.

" And love me, Rachel ? "

" I could not help that if I would," I said,
and went straight from his presence.

CHAPTER XV.

I soon learned that Captain Lambert was a
most determined man when he set his heart on
anything.   It was difficult for me to avoid seeing him, though I managed not to do it again
for several days, except in the presence of
Miss Jane Mandeville.   He sent numerous
messages to me, and, when his arm grew
strong enough, wrote shaky little scrawls on
the leaves of his pocket note-book.   I have
some of those notes yet.   I was going through
a serious struggle during those days, and knew
that it would be best to settle it away from his
influence.   Accepting his love involved a fine
question of honor.   I could not bring myself
to mention Elinor Sims to him, or try in any
way to find out if he meant to deceive me.   His
utter silence puzzled and wounded me.   I loved
him with all my heart; it seemed impossible

for me to give him up, but that was what I
finally determined to do, unless he voluntarily
explained the circumstances of that former engagement. That seemed a very high and noble
resolve, and brought a certain exalted satis
faction; albeit my heart ached grievously all
the time.

In the midst of my perplexity and silent
thinking I did not lose sight of occurrences
around me. Uncle Ned's devices for getting
proper food for his patient were many and cunning. He begged, borrowed, and was often
guilty of stealing, I think. I protested and
scolded, and went so far as to forbid his prowling through the country after nightfall; but
when some stolen delicacy was humbly brought
to me as a peace-offering, I could not fling it
back in his composed and innocent-looking
old face, and accuse him of being a thief. One
night he came in bareheaded, his clothes muddy and torn, and his white wool looking as if
it had gone through a straightening process, it
was standing out so around his black face.

Miss Jane Mandeville and I were sitting in the cabin by a fire, and when he attempted to sidle across the room I detected something under his coat. I also noticed that he panted and trembled as though he had been running.

" Where have you been, Uncle Ned ? " I inquired.

" Oh, jest out a-walkin' for exercise, honey."

" What have you got hidden under your coat ? "

" It's my—my hat, Miss Rachel."

" Let me see it, please."

" Now, honey, ain't I always been hones' an' tru'ful ? What you wanter see my ragged ole hat for ? I done tore it, down in a brier patch. I——"

" Let me *see* it."

He sighed, and looked imploringly at me; then slowly and reluctantly drew a young chicken into view.

" Where did *you* get that ? " I demanded, instantly.

" Roos'in' in de swamp. I 'spect it was skeered

off by de fightin' t'oder day. Anyway, it didn't 'pear like it would be any harm to ketch it."

" You took that chicken from somebody's coop."

" 'Fore de Lawd, I didn't, honey."

" And you were discovered and chased."

" De soldier was, too," he said, with a sly grin. He held the fowl up between his eyes and the light, and looked reflectively at it.

" I 'low it'll be a good br'iler, half o' it for Mars Arnold an' half for you an' Miss Jane. Would you like it br'iled for breakfast, honey ? " in such an insinuating tone that I dismissed him without further words.

It was the next day that Mary Ladislaw came to me, and said that her husband thought it best for us to return to Atlanta. He expected to remain in the hospital until Edgar Sims, who had been wounded in the battle of Chicka-mauga, had recovered, but he wished us to go at once. The duties of a hospital-nurse had worn fearfully upon her. She was blanched and thin, with dark stains under her eyes, and

looked constantly weary. My heart softened
as I looked at her.

"Dear Mary, come up to the loft and lie
down. You need rest. Can we not wait a few
more days?"

She looked at me.

"Is Captain Lambert's wound healing?" she
asked, abruptly.

"Yes," I answered, briefly.

We went silently up the ladder, and she allowed me to tuck her up in bed, then she turned
her head, and said:

"I will ask Henry if we may stay a little
longer."

I kissed her, and went away. When I descended to the lower room, Captain Lambert
walked from the fireplace to meet me, to my
astonishment and confusion. He looked tall
and gaunt, but his moustache and hair had been
freshly trimmed, and he carried himself ever
with soldierly erectness and grace. It gave me
a slight shock to see him in his blue uniform.
I felt alarmed.

" You are surprised to see me out?" he said, smiling, and taking my hand.

" And glad," I could not help murmuring.

" I sat up for the first time three days ago. You would not come to me, Rachel. At last I can come to you. My dearest!"

He would have put his arm around me, but I gently repulsed him.

" You will be made a prisoner, if seen in those clothes," I said, avoiding his eyes.

" I have no others," he replied, in a changed and gloomy tone.

I went on to unfold a plan for his escape through the Confederate lines; wondering, meanwhile, what my friends would say if they knew it. He did not express any gratitude for my forethought, but sat down by the fire, and leaned his head on his hand.

It was a gloomy October day, the landscape a blur of gray mist, and the low clouds flying before an east wind. Uncle Ned stirred the fire into a blaze, and laid on fresh sticks of wood; then, feeling vitally interested in the conversation he sat down on the floor at the end of the hearth. His presence relieved me of embarrassment, as it prevented Captain Lambert from betraying his feelings in speech. It was mingled torture and delight to me to know what emotions must underlie his composed manner. Excitement gave me fluent speech—fictitious brilliancy. I knew he watched me from under his shielding hand, and blushed and paled continually. My plan for his escape was simple enough. Disguised as a Confederate soldier he could go out with Uncle Ned some night on a foraging expedition.

"And what if I am detected, and it is known that you aided me to escape?" he said, rather coldly.

"I will bear all the blame."

"It would redound much more to your credit, as a faithful rebel, to hand me over as a prisoner—your prisoner."

His cold, bitter tone wounded me.

"I am not capable of such treachery!" I cried, rising.

"But you are treacherous to your government, in delivering me from it."

"It is not your place to reproach me with that, Captain Lambert," I exclaimed, hotly. "I am willing to help you escape, but if you prefer imprisonment to freedom, take your choice, by all means: I will leave you to think the matter over."

"Stay, Rachel—Miss Douglas, stay!" he cried, rising and following me; his voice trembling with physical weakness, as well as emotion.

"It 'pears to me like dis fire needs more wood on it," muttered Uncle Ned, and discreetly left the room.

I hesitated. It was not inviting weather for a walk, and I could not make a dignified exit by climbing into the loft again, so I returned to the fire. Arnold came to my side.

"Rachel, why do you behave so capriciously, strangely, toward me? You admitted that you loved me, and I have been counting on the time when I should be released from that infernal bed and could see you, yet you give me no hope, no kindly greeting, even."

"You know what stands between us," I said in a low tone, stealing a swift glance at his face to note the effect of my words. It changed, but not guiltily.

"Is it possible you will let *that* influence you so deeply?"

"I cannot help it, as long as you fail to justify yourself or explain the matter."

"There is no justification or explanation to make. It was simply a question of principle," he said firmly. "I do not repent, though I have suffered, and suffered greatly."

I did not fully understand him, but with my usual rashness supposed that I knew enough to decide my course. Pride and jealousy blinded my good sense, my judgment.

"It has nothing to do with our love, Rachel," he said, softly.

"It has everything to do with it!" I cried, convinced that he intended to deceive me. "You are not free to love me under the cir-

cumstances, and I will not accept happiness
built on such a foundation."

He caught my arm, his pale face turning a
shade whiter.

"Do you mean that you refuse to be my wife?"

"I do."

He turned away and sat down.

"You have never loved me, then."

I made no answer, for already I felt blinded
and choked with tears. I hastily threw on my
cloak and went out into the wet twilight.

It was left to Uncle Ned to secure a grey uniform for Captain Lambert, and the next morning he triumphantly displayed a weather-stained
suit he had stolen from the camp. I held no
more private speech with Captain Lambert for
two days, then he sent word to me that he intended to try to pass through the lines that
night. I spent the day at the hospital, but after
dusk went up to the cabin. New guards were
on around the camp that night, and Uncle Ned
had made the acquaintance of one of them.
The weather had cleared, but it was still wet

under foot and the crisp air was chilling to those of thin blood. Captain Lambert looked terribly ill-fitted for the perilous journey before him, should he pass the picket-lines, and sickening dread oppressed my heart when he came in to bid me good-bye. But I could not persuade him to wait any longer, as, every day, he ran a greater risk of detection. He tried to put on a tone of formality in thanking me, but I stopped him.

"Don't do that."

"It *is* foolish," he said. "It is hard to thank any one in set language for the great gift of life; doubly hard when you love the person who saves you. You like to see me in this garb?"

"I do," I said frankly.

He took my hands.

"Am I to leave you finally, Rachel?"

"Unless you can explain the past more satisfactorily."

"That is impossible. What I did seemed right, and I must abide the consequences to the end. Good-bye."

" Oh, be careful of yourself! " I cried. " It is cruel to think of your facing hardships and perils in your weakened health."

He made no reply, but went from the room, and I heard him speaking to Uncle Ned. I started forward to call him back, but jealous pride held my tongue silent, and their footsteps died away in the rain-soaked earth.

The night crept on, the tedious hours lapsing, one by one, into the past. I kept a lonely vigil, for my friends came in only to seek rest. From time to time I fed fuel to the fire, or looked at my watch. It was midnight when Uncle Ned crept cautiously through the yard and into the room. I sprang up and looked at him as he came within range of the firelight, and read success in his tired face.

" He passed through ? "

" Safe ennuff, honey," a satisfied smile running along his wrinkled cheeks.

" Where is he now ? "

" On his way to Chattanooga, I 'spect. He didn' look fit to take keer o' hisself, he was so weak."

" Did he seem cheerful after passing safely through the lines ? "

The old negro gave me a shrewd, sidelong glance.

" No, honey; he 'pear like a man full o' sorrow."

I went silently up to the loft. Mary lay on the bed, and the candle-light on her eyelids roused her.

" What is it, Rachel ?" she murmured, looking curiously at me.

" Can we go to Atlanta to-morrow ?"

" Are you ready ?"

" Yes ; I loathe this place."

CHAPTER XVI.

HISTORY has dealt fully and justly by the great campaign beginning with the battle of Chickamauga. It is one of the most important in the annals of the war, and displays as much strategy as military skill and power. My pen cannot add anything new to the accounts already given. I spent the early part of the winter at home, the peaceful plantation life a strange contrast to the stormy scenes through which I had just passed. Uncle Ned and I were received and rejoiced over as coming out of the jaws of death, and I know the old man entertained the " quarters" with many a lurid story of adventure and danger in which he prominently figured.

At first my bruised spirit welcomed the security and monotonous tranquillity of the plantation. To lie once more between the smooth lavender-scented linen of my bed, with

Aunt Milly hovering around me; to dine from the old china, every leaf and bud on it associated with some childish memory; to walk and ride with my cousins, or sit in the parlor at twilight and sing for Uncle Charles, with George Washington and some of my own ancestors looking down from their frames in ghostly silence on me, all these familiar things, repeated day after day, made those weeks in the camp-hospital seem almost like a dream. Not quite, though, for I could never forget Arnold Lambert. Through a cloud of distrust and vain regret I saw him constantly. Now that it was all over I could look back with clearer vision, could realize that some misunderstanding must have existed between us. I couldn't tell wherein I had failed to catch his meaning, but the more I thought over those conversations with him, the stronger became doubts of my judgment in the matter.

I had full opportunity for brooding during the idle winter days and long evenings. I had no work to occupy my hands or my thoughts.

It was not necessary to even wait upon myself, with so many slaves about the place, and Aunt Milly jealously watchful to anticipate my smallest desires. Beyond losing two or three men who had run away to join the Federal army, my uncle had not been troubled about his negroes. They remained peaceable and obedient.

But the war had at last laid its hand of terror on the household. Cousin Reuben had been home once on a week's furlough, but had returned to the front again. His letters were necessarily brief and far between, and the haunting dread written ever on Alicia's face was grievous to witness. She said little, but her patient silence seemed more pathetic than speech. Sometimes, when she took her place behind the coffee-urn at the breakfast-table, her eyes would betray the evidence of secretly shed tears, and sometimes they would shine with the calm exaltation of prayer.

She but suffered as thousands of other women all over the country.

It was on the twenty-fourth of November

13

that the battle on Lookout Mountain—since called "the battle among the clouds"—was fought. We first read an account of it in the *Intelligencer*, one of the Atlanta newspapers, then Alicia received a letter from Cousin Reuben from which I quote this passage:—

"The night was intensely dark. We were stationed on Missionary Ridge, and in full view of the battle-ground, but fog and clouds obscured Lookout until after midnight. It was hideous work, fighting in the dark, and I felt doubtful of ever seeing daylight again, but suddenly clouds and mist rolled away and the darkness was illuminated by a lurid blaze of light from the artillery and small arms, and the whole mountain side was like a magnificent panorama. It was a fearful sight, my dear Alicia, but one marvellous to look upon. Every beetling crag and seamy ravine, from the summit of the mountain to its base, seemed to belch forth fire and death. It was like the unveiling of hell before our eyes."

After this battle was fought Alicia and I

read the *Intelligencer* every day, she on account
of Cousin Reuben, and I to see if, by any
chance, Arnold Lambert's name should appear
in its columns. But active hostilities ceased
for a time, and a sigh of relief and thanksgiv-
ing went through the land. In midwinter I
was recalled to Atlanta. The Amateurs had
come together again, and were rehearsing a
new play at the Athenæum. I traveled with
them again, finding diversion but not forgetful-
ness in change of scene and the excitement
of appearing before a new audience every
night. Two vacancies in the company had to
be filled. Lieutenant Devreau was at the front
with the army, and Elinor Sims could not
leave home on account of her grandfather's
precarious health. The first of February we
were in Atlanta again, and the entire company
received an invitation to the wedding of Miss
Sims to Lieutenant Devreau. He had only a
ten-days' furlough, and as the marriage had
been arranged after his arrival in Atlanta,
scant preparations had been made for it.

The news came upon me with a shock, for I had not thought that they would really marry, but after thinking it over, I could not see that it would in any way change my destiny.

They were married in Wesley Chapel just at dusk one evening, and the bride wore her mother's wedding-gown, a silk softly yellowed by time and covered with lace flounces.

" That is her brother," I heard one lady behind me whisper to another, as a pale young soldier walked up the aisle and stood by Judge Lenoir.

" What a pity about the other one ! "

"Oh, they feel it intensely, and are *so* sensitive that they never mention his name."

The beginning of the ceremony stopped the gossip, and I heard no more.

The day after the wedding we went to the reception tendered to General John H. Morgan by the citizens of Atlanta, and heard some brilliant rebel speeches. The feeling had become general that the Federal forces were aiming to capture Atlanta, if possible, but so far the Confederates were still confident of success. Later, when the armies were moving gradually southward, fighting over every inch of the ground, the *Intelligencer* had this to say about the importance of Atlanta:

"Situated as Atlanta is, it is the only link that binds Georgia with the Southwestern States. * * * * With Atlanta in the possession of the enemy, therefore, a powerful blow would be inflicted upon the Southern cause, for Florida would have to succumb at the same time."

The year advanced into spring, and the situation grew more and more serious. Troops were organized for local defense, and general preparations were made for the worst. But the newspapers affected to be still perfectly fearless, and grew sarcastic over the gravity falling like a pall upon the city. I quote from one:

"On the street, every minute, the ravens are croaking. Do you hear them? There is a knot of them on the corner, shaking their heads, with long faces and restless eyes. * * * * But have no fear of the results, for we keep it constantly and confidently before us that General Johnston and his great, invincible satellites are working out the problem of battle and victory on the great chess-board at the front."

A most curious religious phase developed itself that spring and summer. It seemed the direct result of the suspense and anxiety oppressing the people. The churches were open daily, and crowded with devout worshipers, some seeking salvation, others invoking the aid of the Almighty in defeating the encroaching enemy. The ordinary pursuits of life were suspended, or lost all their interest and importance. A crisis was approaching and, human resources failing, a great cry for spiritual help went up from the city daily. The excitement spread among all classes, and it was no uncommon thing to hear prayers and the singing of hymns while passing along the streets.

There was something primitive and touching about it; but, with the battle of Chickamauga

still a vivid memory to me, it seemed utterly
inconsistent to mix the gospel of Christ with
violence and bloodshed; to pray for victory
when it involved a life-and-death struggle between men and brothers. I didn't give expression to my thoughts, but when I prayed it was
not for the overthrow of the enemy, but for
peace.

One day the Ladislaws invited me to drive
with them. We were passing through the outskirts of the city, where tranquillity reigned,
and flower - gardens bloomed with pastoral
freshness, when a dull and muffled boom fell
upon our ears. We exchanged glances, and for
a moment my heart grew faint.

"What is it, Henry?" Mary Ladislaw asked
her husband, her lip trembling slightly.

"Cannon," he said, briefly.

It was the first sound of battle heard in Atlanta. We drove slowly through the streets.
People were coming out on their piazzas, stopping on the corners to listen.

"What is the matter, mamma?" a little child

cried to his mother. She snatched him up, and
went on with blanched face.

We met a soldier.

" Do you hear that ? " he cried to Ladislaw,
tightening his sword-belt, his face excited and
flushed. " They are bound to come, it seems;
but we'll give them such a reception that they
will not stay long."

He walked on with martial tread, lustily
singing a strain from " Dixie."

The next evening, as I came out of a church
at dusk, I met two ladies in the vestibule.
They were both tall and slight and dressed in
black. Their silk mantillas were folded about
their bent shoulders, and old-fashioned bon-
nets, with peaked fronts, covered their heads
and shielded their faces. But I was struck with
a certain familiarity of attitude and outline, and
was in nowise surprised, when they turned toward me, to discover Miss Sarah Ann Mandeville and her sister, Miss Jane. They looked
pale and worn, and had the helpless, bewildered
manner of people set adrift in a strange world.

CHAPTER XVII.

THEY had a piteous story to tell me of the adventures they had passed through since we parted at the camp-hospital. Their home had been destroyed by the invading army, and their slaves were all scattered, except three or four old servants who still clung to them. They were on their way to Augusta, where their relatives lived, but had stopped over in Atlanta and joined the relief corps again.

"We have only our clothes and a few family relics with us," said Miss Sarah Ann.

"And what money we could secrete," added Miss Jane.

"Did they *rob* you?" I inquired, with a shudder.

"The common soldiers, the rabble, confiscated and destroyed everything they could lay their hands on."

"What if they come to Atlanta?" I exclaimed.

"It will be laid waste," said Miss Sarah Ann, solemnly, "laid waste."

"I will not grieve about the property," said Miss Jane; "but when I think of all those niggers we have always been kind to, running away as though they were glad to be free, it makes me indignant. What will become of them without a mistress, I don't know."

"Perhaps they think that they can take care of themselves," I suggested.

She shook her head incredulously, then glided to the subject of their work among the soldiers.

Miss Sarah Ann sighed.

"But it seems so little we can do."

"And the poor fellows need so much care and attention," said Miss Jane.

"Jane was quite broken down last winter, and we had to leave the hospital and go home."

That caused them to wander into reminiscences of the camp-hospitals, and Miss Jane

asked me if I had ever heard anything more of
the Federal officer we nursed in the cabin. I was
glad the gathering darkness hid my changing
countenance from her mild eyes. I hastened
to assure her that I had not. Before we separated I learned where they were stopping, and
promised to see them again in a few days. I
paused on the street corner, and watched them
as they walked slowly away, drawing closely
to each other, as though they felt their solitari-
ness.

The days seemed to hurry by us, each one
bringing the Federal army a little nearer
Atlanta. The city remained quiet. A few
frightened people, who cared not which way
the struggle ended, so they and their personal
property were saved, fled to Canada and other
secure refuges. The *Intelligencer* continued to
give the most hopeful accounts of the situation,
and to express the utmost confidence in Johnston's ultimate victory. It was the policy of the
paper to keep down fear as much as possible.

The Amateurs disbanded again in June, but

I did not leave the city. Now, if ever, the services of both men and women were needed in the defense of the country, and I could not allow my friends to be braver, more self-sacrificing than I. Mr. Ladislaw joined the troops organized for local defense, and Mary and I visited the hospitals daily, where the Mandeville sisters were faithfully at work.

Returning from St. Phillip's Hospital one evening, I passed Judge Lenoir's place, and, leaving my servants at the gate, I ran in to see Elinor (Mrs. Devreau) a few minutes. Since the disbanding of the Amateurs we had not met very often, and after her marriage I seemed to dislike her less than formerly. Personal prejudices were lost sight of, too, in sympathy for the Confederate cause. An impulse carried me in to see her that night—an irresistible impulse. Fate I could have called it. The old negro man who admitted me seemed singularly confused for a well-trained servant. He shuffled his feet, and stammered when I called for Elinor:

" *Is* you come to see Miss Elinor ? " he asked.

"Certainly," I replied, imperiously, "but if she is engaged——"

"I'll—I'll ax her," he stammered, reluctantly allowing me to enter the hall.

The parlor was dark, and I turned toward the library. He clutched helplessly at my arm as I passed through the doorway.

"Not in dar, Miss—honey," he cried; then, seeing that it was too late, threw up his hands with a despairing gesture: "For de Lawd's sake, what is I gwine do now?"

"Go call your mistress," I said, out of all patience with his strange behavior.

"Yes 'm, I is, right now," and he crept down the hall.

The library was divided from Judge Lenoir's apartment by folding-doors. They were pushed back that evening, and only a heavy *portière* hung over the entrance. I heard voices the moment I entered the library. They came from the judge's room. First Elinor's, low and tremulous; then the old man's, excited and harsh:

"It is not worth while to utter one pleading word for him, Elinor. He has forfeited his own honor, and disgraced us. Sir, why have you forced yourself into my presence again?"

"To persuade you, if possible, to leave the city," came in firm tones I instantly recognized as Captain Lambert's. The blood raced from heart to cheek, then back again, leaving me white as a ghost. For my life I could not resist the temptation to approach that *portière*, to lay hold of its thick folds, and draw them sufficiently aside to look into the room. I had no intention of playing the spy, of discovering secrets it was not my right to know. The desire to look once more on Arnold Lambert drew me to the spot.

Judge Lenoir lay on his bed propped up with pillows, his handsome old face flushed with anger, implacable, bitter anger, and Arnold stood at the bedside with Elinor near him, and Mrs. Sims in a chair beyond, weeping hysterically. The old servant was hovering around the door vainly trying to attract Elinor's atten-

tion with frantic gestures.   My eyes fastened on
the two men.

"Yes, it is in keeping with your villainy to
counsel me to play the coward, now that Atlanta is threatened.   What are your plans, may
I ask?" said the judge with a bitter sneer.

"To send you, my mother and sister to New
York," Captain Lambert replied.

I clung to the *portière* to save myself from
falling.   His mother! his sister! could he be
Elinor's brother instead of her lover?

"You will find friends there," he continued.

"Your friends!"

"Yes, and yours, grandfather.   Atlanta is
lost to the Confederacy.   It is only a question
of a few weeks before it will be in our hands,
and I—I want you away from it, grandfather, in
a place of safety."

"Never!" he cried in a resonant tone, lifting
himself from his pillows.   "Begone from my
presence, sir, and never let me see your face
again!   You are the most contemptible thing in
creation, a traitor and renegade!   Think of me

deserting my country in her hour of greatest
need ! "

" My mother and sister, then———"

" Your mother and sister will remain here
with me.   Go !   You could not remember them
when you chose to enter the Federal service.
You were willing to mortify them, disgrace
them, in the eyes of all loyal Southerners by
your conduct."

" Grandfather ! dear grandfather !" pleaded
Elinor.

" Let him hear the truth.   He has brought it
upon himself.   I forbade him this house over a
year ago."

" You know why I entered the Federal service.   It was for the sake of the Union."

" What do I care for the Union ? There has
been no real Union for a quarter of a century.
We have a government."

" But one that must fall."

" Liar ! must you insult me ?"

" Go, Arnold, please go, but don't leave the
house," said Elinor.

"Yes, yes, my darling," wept his mother, wringing her hands distractedly.

He turned once more to the bed, as though to plead for a kinder farewell, but the old man only waved him off with a fierce gesture, then fell back on the pillows, exhausted, laboring for breath. The two women bent over him, applying such remedies for his relief as they had at hand, and Arnold left the room.

I sank into a chair, overcome by the scene and the knowledge that I had made such a mistake. I could see that pride and self-confidence had caused it. I would not allow any one to explain because I felt so sure that I understood the situation. I had condemned Elinor, and heaped suffering on myself and perhaps on him. I heard his steps in the hall, heard him speak to the servant. I sprang up and ran through the room to the door, seized with a frantic fear that he had gone. A light had been placed in the parlor and the old negro stood like a sentinel in the doorway.

"Where is he?" I cried, but he scowled

fiercely and held out a menacing arm. I pushed it aside and ran into the parlor. Arnold sat on the lounge, his face buried in his hands. I knelt before him, clasped his head in my arms, and pressed it against my shoulder.

" Dear Elinor, don't be so grieved. I should not have come. I ought to have known better," he said, with the sound of tears in his low voice. My eyes overflowed.

" It is not Elinor," I whispered.

" Rachel ! " he cried, and lifted his head to look into my eyes; then my face, so near his own, was drawn nearer still. The tears on my cheeks met his.

    *   *   *   *   *   *

" So," he said sadly, when I had explained my presence in the house, " you are sorry for me, Rachel ? "

" More than sorry," I said, tenderly, thinking more of comforting him than of the fact that his feelings toward me might have changed.

" Forgive me; I cannot believe that; I cannot trust in your love, Rachel. At this moment your sympathies are roused, you are soft and tender, but to-morrow——"

"You may trust me *now*," I said, blushing, but firm.

"Why now, more than any other time? Dearest, I am still a soldier in the Federal service, the same conditions exist that——"

"No, no! let me explain!" I cried, and rising and sitting down at the other end of the lounge, I began the story. Before I had said a dozen words he was at my side, listening eagerly; then his arm clasped my waist, and I finished the recital leaning against him.

Elinor came hurriedly in, but stopped with a cry of astonishment. I left Arnold to make explanation to her; then I went up and in my new humility said:

"I don't deserve pardon for wronging you so, but my mean jealousy would not allow me to hear any explanation from you."

She took me into her arms and kissed me warmly.

"I am too glad the mystery is cleared up,

and that you and Arnold are happy, to cherish
any resentment, Rachel."

"How is grandfather?" Arnold suddenly
inquired, a shade of stern remembrance cross-
ing his face.

"He is resting quietly, and mother will be in
shortly."

I dreaded her entrance, but she showed such
pathetic surprise and pleasure that I should
love Arnold in spite of his faithlessness to
country and duty, that I felt sympathy for him
rather than embarrassment on my own account.

"I am proud to love him!" I cried, swept
away out of natural womanly reserve by the
peculiar conditions surrounding us. What I
would have bitterly condemned in another, I
freely forgave in him. Such is the power and
the *injustice* of love.

"My dearest, I wish that I could make you
my wife within the hour!" he exclaimed, lifting
my hand to his lips. "I must be out of the
city again before daylight."

"If Rachel is willing, why can you not

marry ?" said Elinor, eager to do all that she could to promote his happiness.

The proposition coming so suddenly took my breath away. I knew myself to be of age, and capable of using my own judgment, but to decide so serious a matter in a few minutes——

"Why, Elinor !" gasped her mother.

I met Arnold's pleading eyes, and all hesitation vanished.

"Will you, Rachel ?" he whispered. "You owe it to me for being so cruel at Chickamauga."

"Wait! Arnold, wait! How can such a thing be arranged ? If it's known that you are in the city you will be arrested, perhaps shot as a spy!" exclaimed his mother, roused from her usually weak and languid manner by his peril.

"We can trust Mr. Elkin," said Elinor, "and no one else need know it for the present, but Rachel has not spoken yet. Don't let my selfish desire to gratify Arnold's wishes influence you, but if you love him, the sacrifice——"

"Is no sacrifice to me," I interrupted, thrill-

ing with inexpressible feelings of fear and joy.
To be hastily and secretly married had never
entered the wildest, most romantic flights of
my imagination, but it seemed foolish, under
the circumstances, to refuse. I didn't want to
refuse, either.

"Rachel, how I love you for this!" said Arnold, passionately. "Dearest, you shall never
repent it—never!"

I have only a confused recollection of the
next hour. Elinor and Arnold planned the
whole affair; then she ordered the carriage and
went away to make all the arrangements. As
she went out I bethought myself of Uncle Ned
and Aunt Milly for the first time. I ran out on
the piazza, and found them sitting with their
backs to the wall, fast asleep. Elinor sent
them to the servants' quarters.

"Is you gwine to stay all night, too, honey?"
said Uncle Ned, awake and alert in an instant.

"Yes, I have decided to stay," I replied, in
a tremulous tone. I longed to have them in
to witness my marriage. It seemed a little

sad and strange that none of my own people could be with me; but I dared not trust them with the secret.

"Don't you need me, Miss Rachel?" Aunt Milly asked; "co'se you does."

"No, I shall do without your services to-night."

I left Arnold and his mother alone, and went to the room where Elinor had laid out one of her white muslin gowns for me. Mrs. Sims offered to help me dress, but I knew she was longing to be with her son, and declined her services. Alone and unaided I dressed for my own wedding.

CHAPTER XVIII.

IT was a simple task. The borrowed gown did not fit me very well, but it was white and soft—an Indian fabric of silken texture, and easily adjusted. I braided my hair afresh, and fastened a white rose in it. My face flushed and paled; my eyes burned with excitement. I sat down and tried to compose myself; then walked about the room. At one moment I was tempted to go down and tell Arnold I could not be married until a more fitting time and season; the next, I wondered at my own good fortune in being so nearly his wife. Never bride passed through so many phases of feeling in so short a time before. I thought of Uncle Charles and the girls, of Alicia's wedding, of Elinor's wedding, of all the weddings I had ever known anything about, but none of them seemed so strange as mine. The house was silent as the grave. I leaned from the open window and looked out on the city. Sentinel lights flashed here and there; the slow, even tread of a soldier fell on my ears. I raised my eyes, the sky was overcast with a thin veil of cloud—a vapor —through which the stars gleamed faintly, and the moon shone in a watery ring.

"It will rain to-morrow," I was conscious of saying aloud.

All my perceptions were so quickened that the lightest trifles impressed me. I noticed the rustle of the wind through the foliage; and the awakening notes of a mocking-bird, nesting in a tree on the lawn, came to me with piercing sweetness.

A gentle rap on the room-door startled me.

"It is I," said Mrs. Sims's voice; and, when I bade her enter, she came in with a bouquet of long-stemmed bride roses.

"Arnold gathered them in the garden for you."

I blushed, and stretched out my hand for them. They were wet with dew.

"Shall I—shall I wear them?" I said, hesitatingly.

"Carry them in your hand," she replied, after a glance at my toilet.

We stood in embarrassed silence for a moment.

"This—this marriage seems a strange affair, Miss Douglas."

"Do you think I ought not to have consented to it?"

"Oh, no; you understand your feelings best. I only hope it will prove a fortunate one." She came closer to me, laid her hands on my shoulders, and kissed me. "Love him well, Rachel."

I looked at her. Her face seemed strangely old and sad in the candle-light. For the first time I realized that she was Arnold's mother, and soon to be mine.

"Why has he a different name from yours?" I suddenly asked.

"He is the child of my first marriage." She turned the rings musingly on her long, delicate hands. "I cannot blame him so bitterly for fighting against the South. His father's people live in New York, and he has spent several years with them."

"What will Judge Lenoir say when he hears of—that I am Captain Lambert's wife?"

"He is Colonel Lambert now. Oh! father?" —catching at the first part of my question, while a spasm of pain crossed her face—"that you were inveigled into it; that no Southern girl, uninfluenced, would marry him. Father is very bitter." She looked sadly about the room un- till her eyes rested on a Bible. "Have you prayed, Rachel?"

"Prayed? no," I said.

"Then I will leave you until you do. All brides should pray before going to the altar— my daughter."

She said it very sweetly and solemnly, and glided from the room. I knelt down with Arnold's roses pressed to my breast, but before I had composed my mind to a suitable state for prayer Elinor entered the room.

" All ready ? " she cried, her eyes sparkling. " Mr. Elkin is waiting, and I hear Arnold calling us."

Fear seized me like a panic.

" We have been too hasty, Elinor."

" Would you send him away, coldly promising to marry him at the close of the war, provided he lives through it ? What difference can a few months or years make ? Would it not be some satisfaction to know you bore his name, if he fell in battle ? Oh, Rachel, the chances of life in the war are very uncertain."

She took my hand and we silently descended the stairs. Arnold met us at the foot, and drawing my arm through his, led me into the parlor. Strength and courage came back to me. I felt suddenly very calm and collected. There were two gentlemen in the room, one white-haired and of priestly aspect, the other a young man, and, I afterward learned, a great friend of Arnold's.

Elinor closed the doors, drew the curtains more closely over the windows, then we took our places. Mrs. Sims wept gently but quite audibly throughout the ceremony, but no other sound was heard save the voice of the minister. I caught myself listening for the sound of stealthy footsteps in the hall; I noticed the ghostly flicker of the candle-light on the portraits decorating the walls. A few words, a few responses, a prayer and blessing, and I was no longer Rachel Douglas but Rachel Lambert. I was embraced and kissed by my new mother and sister, and congratulated by the gentlemen. Mr. Elkin made out a marriage certificate, and it was signed and given to me.

It was approaching midnight, and the gentlemen soon prepared to leave again. Elinor, who seemed positively gay after the conclusion of the ceremony, pressed them to stay a little longer, and with her own hands brought in wine and biscuit for their refreshment. The clocks of the city struck twelve as they went away. My husband and I had scarcely exchanged a word. We were standing together when Elinor returned to the room, but she pushed him gently away.

" Mother wishes to speak to you, Arnold. I know the time is precious, dear, and that you wish to talk with Rachel. I only want to whisper one word in her ear, then we'll leave you alone."

She drew me to a distant part of the room. " Rachel, do you know why I have so eagerly promoted this marriage ? "

" To please your brother," I said.

" And to keep him with us. He loves you desperately. I saw it at once, and you can exert great influence over him. Use it to the utmost. Command, entreat, weep; refuse to go with him, and assure him that it will break your heart if he leaves you. A man cannot fight against his wife; he must never go back to the Federal service again."

The temptation she presented stunned me. I stared at Arnold sitting on the opposite side of the room with his mother, noted the strength and firmness of his face, and breathed

with relief. I should not be able to move him
from any right purpose or deep-seated conviction; then he raised his glance, met mine, and
smiled with such melting tenderness of lip and
eye, that I feared I could do as I wished with
him.

" What if he refuses ? " I whispered, huskily.

" He will have to leave us within an hour;
run all the risk of being captured, imprisoned,
or shot as a spy; but he will not go, he must
not go, Rachel ! If you love him, you will keep
him with you."

She walked away from me, and she and her
mother left the room. I stood palpitating with
all the fear and shyness of a young girl, as my
husband crossed the room to me. Could I persuade him to remain with me ? He drew me to
a seat at his side on the lounge; took me into
his arms with fond words of endearment. I
leaned, cold and trembling, on his breast.

" It is cruel to have to leave you so quickly,"
he said.

" Must you do it ? " I faltered.

" Yes, or be in such danger as I could scarcely
escape. It was an undertaking of great risk to
come, but I don't regret, now that it has brought
us together—made you my wife."

" Tell me the strongest motives leading you
to enlist in the Federal service," I said at length.

" What, would you spend these last precious
moments in talking of the war ? "

" I want to know what prompted you to fight
against your own country."

" Dearest, I am fighting for my country.
The Southern States represent only a portion
of the United States," and then he gave me a
brief but clear and eloquent account of the
change in his view of the slavery question when
he went North. It was for the preservation of
the Union that he took up arms, that he was
ready to give his life.

" I was tempted to go abroad; to live in Paris
until the agitation was over, the question settled; but that seemed such a cowardly thing to
do that I gave up the thought of it. It has not
been easy to fight against my brother."

" He lay wounded at the same time that you
did," I murmured.

" At Chickamauga ? "

" Yes."

" Every step toward Atlanta has cost me a
pang."

" Give it up ! " I cried, and threw my arms
about him.

" What shall I do, then ? "

" Stay with me," faintly.

He raised my face; looked into my eyes, his
own stern and sad.

" Do you counsel me to do that, Rachel ? I
would then, indeed, be the traitor my grandfather called me."

" No, no; I have been tempted, but I will not
say another word. Do as you think best, Arnold, and I will abide by the decision."

I started up; he rose also, and caught my
hands.

" Rachel, I cannot leave you in this city. I will
send for you, and you must come to me. My relatives in New York will gladly shelter you——"

15

"Nay!" I cried, "be true to the Union, if you wish, but I must also be true to the Confederacy—the South. I will wait for you in my own country, among my own people."

"But how can I lift my hand against Atlanta, knowing that my wife is in it? Rachel, Rachel, what shall I do?"

I was silent, for I knew that if I opened my lips to speak I should say, "Stay and protect me;" I should counsel him against his honor. The temptation to try and hold him at my side had not seemed so strong as at that moment. I sank into a chair, and hid my face in my hands. He caressed my hair.

"Forgive me, dearest, for distressing you so. I will not fight against Atlanta. I can exchange; go to some other post of duty. Look up! we have only a few minutes now. We will speak no more of war, but of love. Do you see this badge?" drawing a ribbon from his pocket, stamped with the colors of the Union. "No matter where I go, if anything happens to me —I mean, if I die away from you—this will come with the date of my death. marked on it."

Half an hour later I knelt by the window in that upper room where I had dressed for my marriage, alone. I did not weep, but the pain of death seemed to hold my heart. Once Elinor came in, but went softly out again. The rosy dawn shone over the city before my vigil ended.

CHAPTER XIX.

MARY LADISLAW was puzzled at the sudden
intimacy which sprang up between Judge Lenoir's family and me. I visited at the house
almost daily, and when I did not go, Elinor
came to see me. It seemed best to keep Arnold's visit to the city a profound secret, so my
marriage could not be published. Elinor did
not reproach me for not keeping her brother,
but I knew she suffered bitter disappointment.

"Grandfather was so proud of him that it
was a terrible blow when he entered the Federal service. We were expecting him home
daily, when the letter came announcing the
step he had taken," she said once, in a moment
of confidence.

We talked about him a great deal, and but
for that and the wedding-ring I wore, I could
have fancied that night a dream, so little

change had marriage wrought in my life. The
wedding-ring had been given by Mrs. Sims,
and it was an opal set in small diamonds. She
had drawn it hastily from her finger during the
ceremony, and then gave it to Arnold. Mary
noticed it on my hand one day.

"A new jewel, Rachel?"

"No, no; an old one, and a gift," I said,
hastily.

She turned it over, watching its mysterious
fire gleam and pale.

"Do you know the old superstition about
opals?"

"Yes; but I am not superstitious."

"I would not care to wear one, though."

I have neglected to mention that, four days
after his secret entrance and departure from
the city, we received a cautiously worded message from Arnold announcing his safe return
to the Federal lines. I carried that slip of
paper in my bosom until it fell to pieces.

The strange experiences I had been passing
through caused my thoughts to turn home-

ward. I felt that I must make known my marriage to Uncle Charles and the girls. I should like, especially, I thought, to talk it over with Alicia. I went over to see Elinor one morning, full of plans for the visit, but I found her reading a letter, and looking very much agitated. Fear clutched my heart.

"Is it Arnold?" I cried.

"No, it is Royal. He has been wounded, and lies in a cabin near Marietta."

I took the paper from her hands—a sheet of the coarse, brown-colored note-paper manufactured by the Confederacy—and read the few lines scrawled upon it. He feared that she would see his name in the list of wounded published in the *Intelligencer*, and wrote to reassure her. His wounds were not dangerous, and the old woman who lived in the cabin took excellent care of him. It was a very cheerful message, but Elinor refused to believe it a true one.

"You may be sure, Rachel, that he is far worse off than he will admit. I must go to him at once."

"I think you are unnecessarily alarmed," I ventured to say, remonstratingly. "I am sure Lieutenant Devreau would not deceive you."

"To spare my feelings he would. You don't realize how great my anxiety is. Then, it seems to me that it is a wife's duty to be at her husband's side when he is ill or suffering."

"How shall we go?"—for already I had decided to go with her.

"Why, will you go with me, Rachel?"

"Certainly; but I warn you that it will be a rough trip, Elinor. Shall we take a private conveyance?"

"I think that would be safer than the railroad."

"What will your mother and grandfather say?"

"Mother is easily managed, and grandfather needn't know it until we are gone."

So for the third time I took an adventurous journey through the country. By paying an extravagant sum of money (Confederate money) we hired a carriage and pair of horses for a week. Elinor packed the roomy old vehicle with fresh bed-linen, rolls of lint and bandages, wine, jelly, preserved fruits, everything she fancied would tempt an invalid's appetite, even to a pair of young chickens.

"Where are we to sit? on the outside?" I inquired, viewing all these preparations with a touch of amusement.

"I thought we might 'scrouge' in," she replied.

At the last moment she ran into the house and brought out a gorgeously colored dressing-gown.

"I intended to give it to grandfather; but I'll take it to Royal."

My two old servants were to accompany us, and soon after noon we started. Uncle Ned was our coachman, and Aunt Milly sat outside with him. It was a very hot day, in the latter part of June, and the dusty roads were baked in the rays of the sun. We were ferried across the Chattahoochee River by an old farmer, who gave us careful directions as to the short-

est and best route to Marietta. He admired
our courage; " But the he'plessness o' wimmen
is thar best pertection," he remarked, sagely.
Then he asked for the latest news from Atlanta, and I gave him a copy of the *Intelligencer*.

" I'm kept that busy with the ferry I ain't
had no time to git in town this summer."

" You have a great many passengers?"

" A sight, a sight o' them. A lot o' fo'ks
air refugeein' before the Yankees—some o'
them tryin' tu save thar niggers." He chuckled
slightly. " I'm mighty glad I ain't got none
ter lose. Ain't you afeard tu take yourn up
thar ?"

" Oh, no," I hastened to say, while Uncle
Ned sniffed scornfully at the bare thought of
deserting his mistress, and Aunt Milly stared
indignantly.

" Sometimes fo'ks cross this ferry that I have
mighty strong doubts erbout," the old man
said, his thoughts taking a new turn. " I rica-
lect one man who wanted tu be put ercross, on
his way tu Marietty, one night, or ruther one

mornin', erbout daylight. He wus er fine-look-in' fellow, but had er twang tu his voice not exactly like ourn, an' I misdoubted he wus er spy o' some sort. He kept his hat down mighty fur over his face, an' paid me in gold 'ste'd o' Confederate money. I tried mighty hard to trip him up with questions, but he had er cunnin' tongue in his head, an' a mind like lightnin' back o' it. He give er fair an' reasonable answer tu ever'thing I said."

"How long ago was this?" Elinor carelessly inquired.

"Several days—mebby two weeks, mebby less."

She and I exchanged glances.

"It must have been Arnold," she whispered.

"I think so."

"Eh? what did yer say?" the old ferryman asked, quickly.

"That your adventures must be very interesting," said Elinor, promptly.

The shadows of approaching evening were lengthening across the forests and fields as we drew near Marietta. We had traveled slowly, and had been stopped several times on the road by the curious country people, who not only wanted to hear the latest gossip from Atlanta, but also our destination. They were dejected and uneasy. They had lived for weeks within the sound of battle, and expected the Federal armies to be upon them at any time. Their corn-cribs and stock-pens had been rifled by the stragglers belonging to Johnston's army, and if their friends robbed them, what would their foes not do? An un-acknowledged desire for peace could be detected in all they said.

The sun had gone down behind Kennesaw Mountain. On parched flower and dusty leaf refreshing dew was already falling, and even our jaded horses seemed to be grateful for the change. Above the earth the air still seemed to glow and palpitate with color and heat, and the outlines of Lost Mountain melted into the summer haze.

" Suppose we throw open the carriage, and

get the benefit of the evening air," I said, as we were driving through a scope of woods.

"If you think it would be safe."

"Surely there is no danger now," I replied. "We have been imprisoned in this stuffy thing all the afternoon. I will speak to Uncle Ned."

Just as I leaned from the carriage window, a squad of men came through the woods. I liked not their looks, and instead of bidding Uncle Ned halt I urged him in a low tone to drive on as rapidly as possible, but they intercepted us and surrounded the carriage. They were our own men, for here and there a ragged grey uniform lent its dignity to the gaunt, hungry-looking crowd.

"Why do you stop us, gentlemen?" I demanded, as boldly as I could.

"What have you got in there?" said one unkempt fellow in copperas-colored jeans, peering through the carriage window. "Oho! somethin' to drink!" his eyes lighting up as they fell on the neck of a wine-bottle sticking out of the hamper at our feet.

They relieved us of all the delicacies Elinor
had prepared for her husband, even dragging
the two terrified and screaming fowls from under the seat. Then they stood respectfully
back and allowed us to drive on. We were
too glad to get safely away to grieve over the
robbery, though Elinor did look disgusted, and
urged Uncle Ned to drive at a break-neck
speed for the remainder of the way. He needed
very little urging, for he and Aunt Milly were
both scared to speechlessness by the soldiers,
or robbers I should say, as they belonged to
the rabble element in the army, and not to the
soldiery.

"To think I should have only this old dressing-gown for him!" said Elinor, after a long
and gloomy silence.

I laughed, feeling quite gay over our escape.

"Be thankful that they didn't take that."

At dusk we drew up before the cabin, after
having gone to various other houses along the
road to inquire for Mrs. Todd. She came to
the door as we entered the gate, and waited,

with her arms akimbo, until we reached the doorstep, when she harshly demanded to know what we wanted.

"Is Lieutenant Devreau here?" Elinor eagerly inquired.

"I ain't sed 'e wus."

"I must see him if he is."

"I ain't sed you could do that, nuther."

"Woman, let me pass! I am his wife," said Elinor, haughtily.

"Why didn't you say that at fust?" cried the old woman, stepping instantly back.

"Elinor, Elinor," cried Royal's voice from the inner room. She ran through the house with a little joyful cry, and I heard her weeping and laughing over him, then the soft murmur of their voices, after the first greetings were ended.

"Ain't you comin', tu?" Mrs. Todd inquired in a softer tone.

"Tell me, first, where we can put up our horses."

"Horses! huh! they'll be tuk afore mornin'.

Don't pester 'bout 'em." She stepped into the yard, and seeing my servants muttered, " More fo'ks ? Let 'em splurge while they kin, they'll not keep thar niggers enny longer th'n thar horses, in these diggin's." She pointed out a small stable across the road. " Thar's whar I kept Joe's filly 'tel hit was stoled. Hit's the unly place I have for stock."

As we returned to the house I explained how we had been robbed of our provisions, and asked if we could have supper with her.

She smiled grimly.

" Hit's mighty pore truck fer sech fine creeturs as you ter eat."

" Anything to stay our hunger will do," I said, as we entered the room.

A pine-knot blazed on the hearth, pouring a flood of rosy light over the bare log walls and sanded floor. The country woman and I took a keen survey of each other. She was a tall, powerful figure, and walked remarkably erect for her age. Her face was brown and wrinkled as a dead leaf, her thin hair almost white. She had large bony hands and a masculine voice. The hard lines of her face relaxed, her stern eyes softened a little as they rested on me.

"Set down an' make yerself at home," she said, gruffly kind, "an' I'll see what I kin git fer yer supper."

It was poor and ill-cooked food we had that night, and Elinor grimaced as we sat down at the bare table, but former experiences had prepared me to accept our situation with a better grace. Before retiring for the night, Elinor informed me that Royal would be able to travel the next day, and we'd take him to Atlanta.

"If the horses are not stolen during the night," I thought.

There was a bed in the outer room and I lay down across it, and watched the fantastic shadows of the firelight playing on the walls and up among the rafters while I thought of Arnold and his possible nearness to me. Uncle Ned and Aunt Milly were lying on the floor asleep, and snoring loudly, and Mrs. Todd sat by the hearth smoking. I finally rose and sat

awhile with her, and she gave me some account
of her life.

" My ole man died twenty year ago, but I
had two sons, two good steddy boys as ever
lived, an' I wus happy ennuff 'tel the war
broke out."

" Where are they now ? "

" Joe wus killed in the battle o' Bull Run, an'
Billy is over thar," nodding her head toward
the Confederate camp. " We didn't have nothin' tu fight fer. We'd no lan' nor niggers tu
defend, but it's on us pore ones the war comes
heaviest, a-robbin' us o' all we have, our fathers
an' husbands an' chillun."

I tried to make her understand that we were
fighting for our rights and liberties, that the re-
bellion was a noble cause, but she shook her
head.

" Slavery's the cause, an' if you'd all a been
willin' tu a give up yer niggers thar wouldn't a
been no fightin'. The lives o' the pore is given
tu save the property o' the rich."

She was too bitter to be reasoned with, or at
16

least that was my conclusion then, so when she
fell into brooding silence again, I rose and
walked abroad in the still summer night. Kennesaw Mountain loomed up against the sky, a
solid black mass lighted here and there with
the starlike glow of camp - fires. Darkness
veiled all the face of the country, but it seemed
instinct with life and motion. Mysterious
sounds vibrated through the air; in fancy I could
see men at work, silently digging trenches,
throwing up breastworks, while others held
consultations, tracing the outline of the plans
for the next day. The watchful sentinel, the
soldier asleep on the ground, the wounded in
the camp-hospital, longing for home and the
healing touch of gentle hands—all, all lay under
that veil of gloom.

I leaned on the fence, surrendering myself to
the thickly crowding fancies, when I chanced
to look down the road, and saw a compact mass
of what appeared to be moving shadows, on it.
At the same instant a hand touched my shoulder and Mrs. Todd's voice whispered in my ear:

"More soldiers comin'. Don't let 'em see you."

We stepped back behind some stunted crape-myrtles sweet with plumy pink flowers, and waited to see whether it was friend or foe approaching.

CHAPTER XX.

THE head of the column drew near, passed by, and with a sigh of relief we recognized the Confederate colors. Such silent marching I never before witnessed. Not a word was spoken, scarcely a footfall sounded on the dusty road. When the last man had vanished in the gloom Mrs. Todd sighed heavily.

" They'll be fightin' agin ter-morrer."

" How do you know?" I whispered.

" Kase they er gittin' ready fer it ter-night. Them men air tryin' tu slip up on the Yankees an' be ready fer 'em in the mornin'."

It was a night of strange wakefulness to me, considering the long drive of the afternoon. Mrs. Todd sat up and smoked, and fed the flame on the hearth with fresh fuel. Once when I woke out of a light, brief sleep, a soldier stood by the fireplace talking in whispers. He went out in a few minutes, tiptoeing elaborately

across the loose, creaking planks of the floor.
The old woman followed him, and I wondered
if he would take our horses.

Morning came at last, and I got up and went
out into the fresh air. It gave me a new sense
of life. There is ineffable charm and loveliness
about a southern summer morning before the
heat of the rising sun steals the dewy coolness
of air and earth. My tired eyes were refreshed
and gladdened by it that morning, and the
morbid fancies of the night all vanished.
Scarcely a sound broke the stillness, except
the singing of birds and the tinkle of cow-bells.
Surely no battle would be fought that day.

The horses were still safe in the stable, and
a certain lightness of heart took possession of
me. It was of brief duration, though. As the
first beam of the rising sun touched the crest
of Kennesaw Mountain, a great puff of white
smoke curled up from the sparse foliage clothing it, and the heavy boom of a cannon startled
the waking countryside. It was on that day
that the battle of Kennesaw was fought.

I saw Elinor standing in the cabin door and hastened to her.

" How is Lieutenant Devreau this morning ? " I eagerly inquired.

"Suffering with fever, but he thinks that by noon he will be able to travel," she said, looking sad and uneasy.

" Oh, I hoped that we could start at once ! " I exclaimed.

The roll of fife and drum smote clearly upon our hearing, and martial sounds of all kinds denoted preparation for battle.

" I knowed what they wus up tu las' night," said Mrs. Todd grimly, as she called us in to a scanty breakfast. " Git erway frum here soon as you can, if yer don't want bloody sights afore yer eyes."

Until noon we were unwilling witnesses of the fight. The cannonading from the top of Kennesaw Mountain was perfectly magnificent, but the time had passed when we could admire such fearful scenes.

" How does it seem to go ? " Royal Devreau

inquired from time to time, excited, longing to
be in the fray.

" I wonder if Arnold is in this battle," Elinor
whispered to me.

I shook my head, unable to speak. The
question had troubled me all the morning.
The fight drew nearer. Once a shell whistled
through the air and fell beyond the house.

" It is hard to be tied to a bed. I can scarcely stand it," grumbled Royal.

" Thank heaven that you are tied to it!" exclaimed Elinor, fervently. "I am not glad
that you are wounded, but I should *die* with
fear if you were out there."

"That is because you are a woman, my
darling, and cannot understand the feelings of
a soldier."

The din of battle frightened Aunt Milly almost out of her senses. She followed me like
my shadow, wringing her hands and distractedly moaning:

" De Lawd God save us, for de end o' de
worl' is comin'! Miss Rachel, make Ned git

dem hosses out, an' let's leave here 'fore we er busted tu pieces. Lawd! Lawd! whar kin a body hide from dem bullets?"

"You is sich a fool, Milly. Now 'f you'd been in as many battles as me an' Miss Rachel—" Uncle Ned began, with the air of a veteran, but she turned on him.

"Shet your mouf, Ned. I ain't gwine to hear none o' your jaw to-day. I'm skeer'd for Miss Rachel, an' I don't keer if I is a fool."

"Miss Rachel! he! he! dat a mighty po' tale, Milly," dodging her fiercely outstretched hand. Privately he asked me to let him harness the horses. I stepped to the door. The rattle of musketry seemed to be startlingly near us.

"It's a-comin'," said Mrs. Todd, grimly. "They'll be a-fightin' roun' the house d'fectly."

She stood in the yard with her hands on her hips. As she ceased speaking a soldier in Federal uniform staggered around the corner of the house. Blood and dust covered his clothes; his face was ghastly pale. He groped blindly for the empty canteen at his side, his parched lips unclosed to utter one word, " water; " then he fell dead at Mrs. Todd's feet. I fled from the horrible sight.

"Come ! " I cried to Elinor and her husband. "We must leave here at once ! I shall go mad or die if we stay any longer! "

Mrs. Todd came in. I begged her to go with us.

" No, my place is here, as long as Billy is over thar fightin'. S'pos'n he'd come as that poor fellow did jest now?" She unfolded a coarse, white cloth, and going out again, spread it over the dead man's face.

Uncle Ned had the carriage before the gate in a few minutes, and we bundled poor Royal into it without much regard for his wounds. But he recognized the necessity for flight, if the Union men were coming. I flung my purse to Mrs. Todd, recklessly munificent in my excitement.

" Drive ! drive ! " I cried to Uncle Ned, as a a body of Federal soldiers appeared at the up-

per end of the road, and he lashed the horses
into a furious gallop. They fired a shot or two
at us, and yelled to us to stop, but we continued
our flight until the poor horses were in a lather,
and Royal fainted from the swaying motion of
the carriage. All danger was past, and we
traveled the remainder of the way at a more
reasonable pace.

Late that afternoon we rolled into Atlanta
again, but the half-day of hot and wearisome
travel had thrown Royal Devreau into a high
fever. His wounds had reopened, and he talked
deliriously. He was borne to bed, and lay
there for weeks before he could be pronounced
out of danger. Elinor could scarcely leave his
bedside, and, knowing how her grandfather
would miss her, I devoted myself to him. He
was able to go out again, and many an hour
we spent on the shady piazzas, while I read to
him or we talked war-news. A threefold purpose I had in winning his regard: to make myself useful, to spare Elinor, and to reinstate my
husband.

At first Arnold's name was never mentioned between us, but one day, after considerable confidence had been established, he spoke of his recreant grandson. It was with mingled shame and bitterness.

"I suppose you have heard of him?"

"I have," I replied, "and more than that, Judge Lenoir, I have met him."

He was astonished.

I hastened to tell him of that first encounter in the mountains, and the gallant way Arnold rescued us from the outlaws, then the meeting with him at the Montgomery place. There I stopped and looked at him. His face had hardened, but I could detect a certain eager interest in his eyes, and went on to tell of Chickamauga.

"There is more yet," he said, when I again paused. "Go on."

"I don't know that I dare."

"What!" he cried, striking his stick on the floor, "has he been guilty of——"

"I am his wife," I said in a low tone, but proud to say it.

He fell back in his chair, and stared speech-lessly at me. Hurriedly I explained the cir-cumstances, and dwelt strongly on my love for him, and the happiness it gave me to bear his name.

"And," I concluded, laying my hand timidly on the arm of his chair, "and so I am really a member of your family."

"But—but I disowned him," he stammered, evidently in doubt how to take the situation.

"I suppose you don't care to have my society any longer, then?" I said, gently and sadly.

"Good heavens, child! sit still, and let me have time to think. I cannot, you know, I can-not forgive him for the disgrace he has brought upon us, but you—you are not to blame for his misdeeds. I don't understand how a loyal woman could marry a man so disloyal——"

"Love does not consider political principles," I said, boldly. "Arnold is as honest in his con-victions as we are in ours."

"A woman is always the echo of her hus-band. I am afraid that you will live to repent this marriage. It was a most rash step to take. What pleasure can you hope to derive from it ? "

" The war cannot last forever," I said, hopefully.

I continued my attentions and ministrations to him, and he accepted them as from one of his family. Arnold's name came up often in our talks, but the old man refused to pardon him.

During this time the most intense excitement prevailed in Atlanta, for the Federal armies were drawing nearer and nearer the city, with every intention of capturing it. The sounds of conflict became as familiar as the traffic on the streets. It was singular and pathetic that the first shell thrown into Atlanta should kill a little child, but do no other damage. It was a great shock to the whole city. The panic-stricken people ran about the streets with pale faces, or stopped in groups to discuss it. We felt, then, that the enemy was indeed upon us, and the wise and prudent made prep-

arations for a siege, building bomb-proofs and
storing provisions.   What fabulous prices we
paid for the simplest articles, and thankful to
get them !—twenty dollars a pound for coffee,
and three hundred for a barrel of flour.   I paid
fifty dollars for a coarse pair of shoes for Uncle
Ned, and felt proud of my bargain.

Two days after the first bomb was thrown
into our midst the battle of Atlanta was fought,
and the siege began.

CHAPTER XXI.

To give an account of half the incidents and accidents occurring in Atlanta during the siege would fill a volume. Tragedy and Comedy stalked side by side, and there were people who could laugh as well as weep over the situation. Two railroads to the southwest were still open, and trains loaded with refugees rolled out of the city daily.

I was cut off from all communication with my relatives, as the Federal armies lay between us, and suffered many pangs of anxiety concerning their fate. After the first panic of fear was over, Atlantians—those who intended to cling to the city to the end—settled down into comparative calmness again. The streets, deserted in the first days of the siege, were again peopled; and instead of flying into a bomb-proof every time a shot was fired we learned to dodge the missiles of death, and go on.

The last entertainment that the Amateurs
gave was at a town below Atlanta. The train
that we went out on was shelled, and one of
the bombs fell into our car. Without an instant's hesitation, Henry Ladislaw snatched it
up and flung it out through a window, and we
heard its dull explosion as we rolled away.
That night was the last the Amateurs ever
played together. The next day Royal Devreau, who had recovered from his wounds,
returned to army duty, and we to the painful
uncertainties of life in the besieged city again.

It was impossible to learn anything that was
taking place outside of the fortresses of the
city, and equally impossible to get a correct
statement of the situation from any one inside.
A thousand rumors were afloat; a thousand
conflicting stories told. If the firing ceased
for an hour or two, it was said that the Federals had thrown up the siege, and were in full
retreat; or, if the shelling was heavy, that
they intended to literally wipe the city out of
existence with their big guns.

The newspapers—and they were numerous, many of them having been driven southward in advance of the Federals—gave the most flattering reports of the situation, daily, as well as many of Hood's officers. It seemed to be the policy of editors and soldiers to keep the people hopeful.

Every morning I read the journals to Judge Lenoir, and he would grow exultant for a few hours. It enraged him to have to seek protection in the bomb-proof cellar.

"For all the world like rats in a hole!" he exclaimed. "If I was not so confoundedly old and crippled, I would show them what one man could do!"

"What would you do, grandfather?" Elinor inquired, cheerfully.

"I'd blow as many of them into perdition as I could pull the trigger on!"

"I think, father, that we ought to pack up our valuables, take the servants, Elinor—and Rachel, if she will go with us—and refugee to Macon," said Mrs. Sims.

17

" No; we will stay here, *here*, Lizette, until we are driven out. I don't propose to run away."

" But if the city surrenders ? "

" It will not surrender. I am not afraid of the result of this siege. The Yankees will be ready to give it up when they find that it will not accomplish anything. Remember, Edgar is here."

" Do you think I can forget it ? " she cried, reproachfully.

" Then don't talk of leaving."

" And I could not leave Royal," said Elinor, quietly but firmly.

There was no special tie binding me to the city, except my friends. I had not heard a word from Arnold since those few lines on his departure from Atlanta, and often the suspense seemed intolerable. On the urgent entreaty of his relatives, I went to live with them, though my marriage still remained a secret outside of the home-circle. Edgar Sims felt exceedingly bitter against his brother, but

Royal Devreau displayed a more tolerant
spirit. They all pitied me, I knew, though
Arnold's name was rarely mentioned, except
by Elinor.

The long summer days passed very slowly,
in spite of the excitement. As a vent to my
feelings, I took to writing poetry — various
pieces appearing in the *Intelligencer*, and other
papers. To quote from Reed's *History of Atlanta*, recently published:

" In such stirring times the literary faculty
of a people always undergoes a rapid and ab-
normal change. When the issues of life and
death are in the very air; when every man is
stimulated to deeds of heroism and self-sacri-
fice, there is a fever in the most sluggish veins,
and the dullest man talks and writes in a picturesque and graphic style. In the army and
out of it, men and women who had never
thought of writing for the press rushed into
print with letters, stories and poems, so emotional, strong and fiery that they cannot be

read without a thrill of excitement, even at
this late day."

I can testify that authorship was a relief to
the intensity of my feelings. We were not
without new publications in Atlanta, in the way
of books, though they were often printed on
the coarse, brown paper used in butcher-shops.
I read *Les Misérables* printed on wall-paper.
Just as people rushed into print, so they read
—many of them who had never cared at all for
books.

*   *   *   *   *

The city had grown comparatively quiet,
and we crept out of the stifling cellar into the
cooler, fresher air of the house above. It was a
sultry August evening, and as we had been
imprisoned most of the day I proposed to take
my servants and walk over to see the Ladislaws. The two old negroes were very unwilling to venture out on the street. They had
been in a state of abject terror ever since the
beginning of the siege, and spent most of their
time in the cellar.

I found Mary alone—her husband having gone out into the city to learn latest reports of the situation. She had not lost hope, and talked in the most serenely confident way of our ultimate victory over the Federals. I could not share her opinion, but went away feeling better for the visit.

As I returned home several fuse-shells were fired, passing across the sky with a lurid trail of light behind them.

"*Lawd!* dey're at it agin!" groaned Uncle Ned, in accents of despair. "Miss Rachel, we'd better be a-gittin' home quickly ez we kin. When dem shells gits ter bustin', 'tain't no tellin' whar dey gwine ter fly an' light."

I was watching the course of one of those shots from a street corner, when a husky voice addressed me in very good French. I looked around. An old man, in rather shabby citizens' clothes, stood at my side. He leaned on a stick, a long, white beard flowed down over his breast, and long, white hair fell from under his hat-brim to the collar of his coat. He was tall, but stooped slightly, and his eyes seemed to pierce me with their intense gaze. My knowledge of French was limited to the reading of very simple books.

"Will you not speak English?" I said, in some confusion.

"May I trouble Madame to tell me the way to the Trout House?" he said, with a bow.

The Trout House was the principal hotel in Atlanta at that time. I told him as clearly as I could how to reach it.

"I have just arrived in the city," he continued.

"You have selected a most ill-omened time for your visit," I said, dryly.

"It is dangerous, isn't it?"

"Very," I said. "If you don't care to spend most of the time in a cellar or dugout, I would advise you to take the first train from the city."

He stroked his beard with a sinewy, youthful-looking hand, and I heard him sigh.

"Have you been greatly troubled, madame?"

" Every Atlantian is more or less troubled,"
I said. " The situation is one of constant peril,
but you will discover that before the night is
over. Remember to turn at the next corner,
and you will easily find your way to the hotel."

He bowed, murmured his thanks, and I
continued my walk. Curiosity impelled me to
look back when some distance away. The old
man still stood at the corner, leaning on his
stick.

When I reached Judge Lenoir's gate, Uncle
Ned pointed out a solitary figure across the
street. The stranger had followed us. A thrill
of fear ran through me. The times were so
fraught with agitation; so many strange and
lawless deeds were perpetrated in the city, that
the old man's movements seemed very suspi-
cious. I sent Uncle Ned and Aunt Milly away
to bed, but I sat down on the piazza, behind a
screen of vines to watch and wait a few minutes. If robbers threatened the household,
they should meet with a warm reception.

I saw the stranger slowly cross the street

and open the gate. He closed it softly; then stepped out on the grass, to avoid the hard, paved walk leading up to the steps. My heart gave frantic leaps of terror. I stood up, clinging to the vine-wreathed column. It seemed a foolish courting of danger to remain there alone, but I was incapable of flight.

The stranger mounted the steps lightly and quickly, dropping his cane on the grass below. Courage came back to me. He started, slightly, as I met him.

" Sir, what do you want here at this unseemly hour ? " I demanded, sternly.

" You," was the unexpected reply. Then he seized my shoulder, my waist, in a strong, gentle grasp. " Rachel, darling—darling ! "

The scream on my lips changed to a sob; for a moment, I think joy bereft me of consciousness as I recognized my husband.

* * * * *

" And so you didn't recognize me when I spoke to you on the street ? " Arnold said, when we sat down on the bench behind the

vines. His disguise had been thrown aside
for a short time.

"Could I have talked with you so calmly if
I had?"

"I could hardly resist snatching you into
my arms, when you so sweetly and coolly answered my questions. It was a good test to
my disguise. If you didn't recognize me, there
is no danger of detection."

I drew his head down and kissed him, passing my hand caressingly over his hair. I still
felt half dazed.

"Is it real—is it real, or only a blessed
dream?" I whispered.

"My dearest, have you suffered so?"

"The suspense was terrible! If I could have
heard occasionally from you!"

"You shall go with me this time, Rachel; I
have written to my relatives in New York, and
they will be glad to receive you."

"I don't want safety while you and my friends
are in danger. It is useless to ask me to leave
Atlanta, Arnold, while your family remain."

He pleaded and argued. I saw how his heart was set on it, and it hurt me cruelly to distress him, or to refuse to yield to his wishes, but my whole being revolted against such an arrangement.

"Don't be angry with me, Arnold, but it is as impossible for me to leave the South, Atlanta, at this time, as it is for you to become a rebel," I said, piteously; tears streaming down my face.

He instantly took me into his arms again.

"Dearest, forgive me. It is only my great anxiety about you that causes me to seem so cruelly persistent."

"Why did you not exchange as you thought you would?"

"Because it involved such a separation from you, Rachel. As long as I remained in this part of the country there would be at least the hope of seeing you. I would try to exchange to-morrow if you were out of Atlanta."

The front door was pulled softly open, and Elinor appeared in dressing-gown and slippers.

"Rachel! Rachel!" she called in a subdued tone. "I thought I heard her voice," she continued to herself.

"Come out, Elinor," I said. "We have a visitor."

Arnold stepped out from behind the vines, and she ran into his arms.

We took him into the house, stealing through it like thieves, for fear of disturbing Edgar and the judge. Elinor flew to wake her mother.

The visit from him could not be one of unalloyed delight. Elinor and his mother entreated him with tears to remain in the city, and it wrung my heart to see how deeply it distressed him to refuse.

He remained with us until just before daylight.

"When can you come again, Arnold?" his mother inquired, bursting into tears when he rose to take leave.

"I don't know, mother!" he replied sadly, bending to kiss her.

I followed him to the piazza.

"I think it will be best for me not to come

again," he said to me when we were alone.
"It is more sorrow than joy to see me. Poor
mother! Be a good daughter to her, Rachel!"

I clung to him; my heart riven with the anguish of parting.

"Come, do come again!" I pleaded. "To
me it is life to be with you; death to be separated from you."

I will not linger over those last moments.
Through blinding, bitter tears I watched him
go down the walk, and away along the deserted
street, once more transformed into an old man
leaning on a staff.

CHAPTER XXII.

CHANGES were rapidly approaching. It was
about the middle of August that we had the
most terrific day of all the siege. It was the
day of the artillery duel. We breakfasted in
the dining-room that morning for the first time
in several days. The Ladislaws had been invited
over to join us, and Edgar and Royal were at
home.

The grape-arbor, partly destroyed by an ex-
ploding shell, still had vines enough clinging
to it to yield grapes for the feast, and a bowl of
roses bloomed in the centre of the table.

We made quite merry over the meal, for to
be always sad seemed unnatural and impossible.
Arnold's secret visit had lightened my heart
wonderfully, and when Mr. Ladislaw asked me
to go into the parlor and sing for them, I readily
complied. He sat down at the piano, and played
a gay and graceful prelude.

" What shall I sing ? " I asked.

Before he could reply the booming sound of Federal guns saluted us, and a shell passed over the house. I turned white, but he played on undisturbed, and finally said:

" Sing a verse or two of ' The Canteen,' then I want to hear that pretty and sentimental ' Would I Were with Thee.' He struck into a lively accompaniment, and I sang:

" There are bonds of all sorts, in this world of ours;
　　Fetters of friendship, and ties of flowers,
　　　　And true-lover's knots, I ween;
　　The girl and the boy are bound by a kiss,
　　But there's never a bond, old friend, like this—
　　　　We have drunk from the same canteen.

" We have shared our blankets and tents together,
　　And have marched and fought in all kinds of weather,
　　　　And hungry and full we have been;
　　Had days of battle, and days of rest,
　　But this memory I cling to and love the best—
　　　　We have drunk from the same canteen."

He joined in when it came to the last verse, his bold, rich voice filling the house with melody, and the negroes crowded in the hall,

delighted to hear the sound of music once more.
For an hour we hovered about the piano, trying our old music, but the batteries inside as
well as outside of the city had opened fire, and
war held supremacy again. Mary spent the
day with us; indeed, it would have been dangerous for her to go out on the street; for over
the city, so calm in the dawning day, blazed
and roared a thousand shots. We sat in the
dark cellar with the terrified servants huddled
about us, thinking of those exposed to the pitiless firing, silently praying, even while we tried
to cheerfully talk. Would the lagging hours
never pass? Would that hideous uproar din on
our aching ears forever?

The day passed its noon. Once, in a brief
lull, Elinor and I crept up-stairs and gathered
together all the food we could find, to take
back to our retreat. The atmosphere was
thick with smoke and the fumes of powder; the
sunlight had the lurid glow of fire.

Elinor clung to my arm with white face and
terrified eyes as a shell struck the stable at

the back of the garden, and scattered it in
fragments on the ground. She seized a plat-
ter of bread and fled back to our underground
retreat. I started to follow her with a tray, on
which I had flung meat, pickles and the fruit
left from our gay morning repast, when the
hall-door was thrown open, and Miss Jane
Mandeville entered, her bonnet awry, her mantilla trailing over one shoulder.

" Feel of me, Rachel! see if I have all my
limbs!" she cried, when I ran out into the hall.

" Why, what is the matter, Miss Jane?" I
exclaimed, seizing the gentle, trembling creature in my arms. Her face was blackened with
powder-smoke, and the tears, trickling down
her cheeks and over her nose, left queer lines
and smirches. It was not a time to laugh. My
own eyes smarted with sympathetic moisture,
and a hysterical choking filled my throat; but
for all that, a convulsion of mirth passed over
me.

" I—I feel singed; I don't know but I feel
blown up!" she said, with a piteous sob, ren-

dering the condition of her face more gro-
tesque still by trying to wipe away the tears
with a corner of her mantilla.

"How did it happen? I am sure that you
are uninjured, except for some holes scorched
in your dress," I said, loosening her bonnet-
strings and smoothing her disheveled hair.

"I had just crept up-stairs, and put on my
bonnet, for Sarah Ann went to the hospital
this morning, and I promised to be with her
by noon, when, the first thing I knew—well, I
didn't seem to know *anything* very clearly until I was on the street, running. My room was
torn to fragments; half the house was shattered."

"Rachel, why don't you come down?"
shouted the judge, impatiently; "don't you
know that you are in danger? We can do
without food, if that is what you are trying to
get."

I led Miss Jane down into the cellar, where
she was greeted with exclamations and many
expressions of sympathy. She had had a very

18

narrow escape, and the shock had left her weak and nervous. She refused to join us in our scanty repast, but reclined on a bench, sighing hysterically, and occasionally describing some particularly vivid sensation of pain or terror seizing her as she ran wildly through the streets.

We were none of us very anxious for food. Our table was an upturned box, and we were surrounded by trunks, pictures, and a miscellaneous collection of furniture. Many things had been removed from the upper part of the house, and stored in the cellar for safe-keeping, in case shells should destroy the building. The afternoon passed very much as the morning had. Judge Lenoir walked up and down the narrow space left vacant between the window and the stairway, and we huddled together, or reclined on bales of goods, while the very foundations of the world seemed to shake and totter.

"I think they've turned hell loose on us," the judge said once, as a more than usually deafening explosion took place. The house trembled and rocked; bricks fell from the cellar wall, and the stifling fumes of burning powder made us gasp for breath. The negroes burst into loud lamentations, calling on God to save them; and Mrs. Sims clung to Elinor.

I dashed up the steps and found the left wing of the house in ruins. It gave me the strangest sensation to see the murky daylight shining through the shattered walls of the dining-room. I shuddered as I thought what a short time had elapsed since Elinor and I stood in the room.

The poor, terrified negroes fell prostrate to the floor when I gave an account of what had happened, and it required Mary Ladislaw as well as Elinor to soothe and reassure Mrs. Sims. Miss Jane was still absorbed in her own exciting experiences, and heard the news quite calmly.

"I am sure our fragments will be scattered all over the city before night," she said, in a resigned tone. "There'll not be a whole body left amongst us."

The judge insisted on going up and seeing the extent of the damage; and I accompanied him. Broken china and furniture lay scattered about, and we picked up several pieces of the silver from the *débris*. But it was too dangerous to linger around the wreck. Shot and shell whistled through the air in almost every direction, and we beat a hasty retreat.

At last nightfall put an end to the work of destruction, and we could venture forth into the open air again. Mrs. Sims sat down and cried over the wreck of her household goods, the rare old china, the porcelain jars, and all the dainty wares collected through generations of wealthy householders, and cherished for the sake of associations as well as commercial value.

Miss Sarah Ann Mandeville came in soon after the firing ceased, and it was pathetic as well as a little comical to see the sisters embrace and weep over each other.

"When I found the house had been destroyed, I searched among the ruins for your body;

then I feared that your mangled remains had
been blown entirely away," said Miss Sarah
Ann, mournfully.

"I ought to have gone to the hospital, but I
was that frightened, Sarah Ann, I didn't have
any sense, and when I got here they would not
let me leave again," said Miss Jane, contritely.
"I knew you would be anxious, would naturally expect to find me in a fragmentary condition."

"It was to save you that sad experience,
Madame, that we insisted on keeping your sister with us," said the judge. "She had one
miraculous escape, but we could not hope for
two in one day. I hope you will make this
your home until you have time to develop new
plans. It is not much of a home now," waving
his hand toward the wrecked portion of the
building, "but such as it is we'll gladly share
it with you."

They were profuse in their expressions of
gratitude, and accepted the hospitality so
frankly offered.

It was said that very little was accomplished
by that day's cannonading, that only a lot of
ammunition was wasted, but, not counting the
destruction of property in the city, and the loss
of other lives, for many citizens, men, women,
and children were killed and wounded, one
noble, gallant Southerner, who could ill be
spared, was sacrificed—Henry Ladislaw. He
went from us that morning with a song on his
lips; he came back borne on a stretcher, pallid
and with the shadow of death already falling
upon him.

I will pass over the dismay and grief of such
a coming. We stole noiselessly about, talking
in awe-struck whispers, each with some tender reminiscence to tell of the brave and gifted
leader of the Amateurs. He alone seemed to
have naught to regret.

"It is a glorious death to die, Mary," he
said in faint tones, smiling when his wife bent
speechlessly over him. He gathered her
hands against his wounded breast. "I die for
my country."

"But to leave me alone! How shall I remain here without you, Henry? Oh, my heart's love, my heart's love! take me with you!"

Across his face came a spasm of pain. As she sank to her knees by the bed, and buried her face in the pillows, he raised one hand and laid it caressingly on her head.

"Your loyalty is indeed put to the test, Mary. 'Tis my sole regret in dying that I must leave you."

It was the first and last outburst of her grief that she permitted to disturb him. A soldier's wife must be heroic if she can stand at his side through the perils of war, and then see him die without a plaint. Mary Ladislaw's heroism and unselfishness never shone in such a beautiful light as they did during the watches of that night.

None of the household slept except the servants. About twelve o'clock Ladislaw called me.

"Sing for me, Rachel," he said, smiling. "I should like to hear some of the old favorites once more."

I sat down at the piano in the next room and softly played and sang the war ballads we had been wont to enliven the Amateur programmes with, while my tears fell thick and fast on the ivory keys, and my voice grew tremulous. It was a strange hour for music, and it echoed weirdly through the silent house. Once or twice the wounded man tried to join in some particularly inspiring strain, but his voice rose scarcely above a whisper, and he sank back exhausted.

It was a long time before I could touch the piano again without so vividly recalling that night and its sorrowful experiences, that it was pain instead of pleasure to me to play or sing. Later in the night his mind wandered. He talked of the Amateurs, planned new programmes, hummed new melodies he intended to use.

"But perhaps I ought to be on the field. Mary, can I do more good, fighting, than earning money for the soldiers? I want to do my whole duty, to go where I shall be of the greatest

service. A letter from Edward. He sets my
doubts at rest. It is true, all men are not
gifted alike. He says that I am using mine in
the noblest way. Hark! what was that? the
roll of drums? Another victory has been won.
Let me sing it aloud."

He seemed to live over again all the trying
experiences of the war. Once he spoke regret-
fully of so lavishly giving all his own property.

" But Mary said, ' Do it.' How will she live
if I am taken ? "

" Have no fear," she whispered soothingly.

He started, the sound of her voice bringing
him back to himself.

" Are you here with me, Mary ? Sweet, I am
glad for your sake that the hour has not yet
come."

" What hour, my beloved ? " she said, with a
sob.

" The hour of separation."

Toward morning he fell into a trance-like
state, and we saw that the hour was quickly
coming. Just before daylight he suddenly

roused as from a dream, his eyes opening
widely, brilliantly. He held out his arms to his
wife.

" Lift me up, Mary. I want to see the light.
It is the new day, Mary, the new day dawning
for the South—our beloved South. It will be a
long time before you can see it. The darkness
will thicken—clouds and storm will obscure the
first gleams of light, but beyond it all lies
peace, prosperity, the clear shining of the sun.
Strange, strange that it does not come as we
would have it! *Ours—is—a—lost—cause !*"

He spoke clearly at first, looking toward the
eastern window where all was still darkness to
our eyes, but on the last words his voice failed.
He turned and gazed on his wife's face; his
hand groped for hers. When his head sank
against her shoulder we laid him gently down
again, and as we did so his eyelids closed; rigid
repose sealed his lips forever.

CHAPTER XXIII.

THE influence of Henry Ladislaw's death was felt far beyond the limits of our small circle, but the times were too full of dread suspense, of intense excitement and change, for a friend to sorrow long outwardly for a friend. Too many were passing through the dark valley, to linger by one bier. To-day a fallen hero was wept over, to-morrow, perchance another. It is reserved for only a few to be mourned by a whole nation.

Ladislaw filled a place peculiarly his own. No other in the Confederacy, I think, could have kept an amateur troupe of players together so long, or raised so much money, but his work in that direction had ended before death set him free from all earthly service.

Mary had relatives living in Savannah, and after her husband's death they sent for her.

Life had lost all hope or interest for her. Grief had not stunned, but made her indifferent, alike to her own fate, and to the fate of the Confederacy. Ladislaw's last prophetic words had made a deep impression on her.

" But success or failure will have little effect on me now," she said once to me.

I could not utter any of those platitudes and set conventional phrases we always seem to hold in reserve for our afflicted friends. Her calm tone carried such conviction of the truth that I could only acquiesce.

She went away, and in a few days other impressions began to crowd her sorrowful image into the background. We were cut off from all communication with the outer world about this time, and fears for personal safety seized the imprisoned people. As long as a way of escape from the city was open, no such panic was felt. The suspense did not last long. The battle of Jonesboro' was a decisive one. It settled the fate of Atlanta. For that reason I have cause to remember it, as well as for a more

important one. I will attempt no account of
this battle. The day it was fought was an
anxious one for Atlantians. The general belief was that we were winning the victory, but
no certain or reliable information could be
gained that day or the next, though it became
known in an indefinite way that the rebels had
suffered defeat. The day after the battle was
one of greater anxiety, even, than the one on
which it was fought. We heard nothing from
either Edgar or Royal, and Elinor and her
mother were both deeply troubled. Subdued
but unusual activity reigned in the military
quarters of the city. What it meant we could
not tell.

"Surely they don't intend to give Atlanta
up?" I said once to the judge.

"Tut, tut, child! of course not!" he testily
replied, but he paced about the hall and piazzas
all day, and I could see that he shared the
general feeling of uneasiness. Night again fell
without bringing either of the young men.
Elinor and I sat on the piazza long after the

other members of the household had retired.
It was a great relief to be freed from the dangers of flying shot and shell from Federal batteries, and strange, after weeks of siege, but
whether greater dangers threatened we could
not say.

Stifling clouds of dust hung in the sultry air,
raised by the constant passing of wagons along
the streets. Elinor and I talked a little in low
tones, but for the greater part of the time kept
silence. Deep, inexpressible sadness weighed
upon us for the changes which had taken place,
and for those yet to come. We had fallen into
very sisterly intercourse. She and the judge
were my favorites in the household. To neither
Mrs. Sims nor Edgar could I feel very closely
drawn. "The dangers of the battle-field cannot be more cruel than the suspense of those
who stay at home," she said to me after one of
those long silences. "At this moment, Royal
or Edgar, or both, may be dead or wounded,
and yet we must sit here and patiently await
the tardy coming of news."

"But it *will* come," I said, with a sigh. "Your fate is not so hard as mine, for if Arnold has been killed I have no way of finding it out."

"Oh, don't speak of it!" she exclaimed with a shudder. "I cannot bear any more, Rachel."

An ammunition wagon lumbered by the gate.

"Can they indeed be leaving us?" said Elinor, grasping my arm. We stared at each other through the gloom, helplessness, deadly fear expressed in that gaze. To be deserted by our army, given over into the hands of the enemy! It seemed a terrible fate. One hope sent the blood flying back to my cheeks. "Arnold will save us," I said.

A long line of army wagons rolled along the street. The judge came from his room through the parlor, and leaned from the front window.

"What is it going on out there?" he asked.

"The city is being evacuated," said Elinor.

"Impossible!" he cried, and came out to the piazza. "Ha! a man is entering the gate. Perhaps he can tell us what this means."

" It is Royal ! " Elinor screamed, starting up,
and in another moment was in her husband's
arms.   He looked dusty and haggard, but had
no time to spare to take food or rest.   He gave
a hurried account of some of the disasters of the
battle, and acknowledged that the army was in
full retreat.   By morning the city would be in
possession of the Federals if they chose to
come and take it.

The news stunned us, but I felt buoyed up
by the secret hope that when the Federal army
came I should see Arnold.

The judge walked the piazza, his head sunk
on his breast, silenced and crushed by the evil
tidings.

" Sir, I hope that you will leave the city at
once," said Devreau.   " I cannot remain with
Elinor, and it is very trying to think of leaving
her here."

" *I* will protect her.   No man can molest the
women of my household as long as I live ! "
exclaimed the judge, fiercely, smiting his
breast with a feeble, tremulous hand.   We knew

that the spirit was strong and brave, but what
could an old man do?

"And your grandson will, of course, extend
his protection. I had forgotten him," said
Royal, brightening visibly. It was a most un-
fortunate speech. "I would be garroted rather
than accept a favor from him!" said the old
man in a rage. "Don't insult me by the mention of his name!"

No one made any reply, but three pairs of
young eyes exchanged sympathetic glances,
and I knew Royal felt satisfied that Elinor and
I would profit by Arnold's presence, should he
come into the city.

He had to join his command in a short time.
It was painful to see him go again. Elinor
broke down and sobbed passionately at the
last moment. He turned and waved a farewell from the street before disappearing in the
file of soldiers marching by. Edgar had sent
messages by his brother-in-law. He was safe
and well, but could not get away to come to
the house.

19

The night wore on, but we couldn't think of
sleeping. The city continued in a turmoil of
moving troops, wagons and artillery, until the
middle of the night, when quietness settled
down over the deserted streets. It was not
destined to last long. I had gone to my room,
and was sitting by the window, when a series
of the most terrific explosions shook the house
from roof to basement. The windows shattered, splintered glass falling indoors and out,
pictures dropped from the walls, and a chimney in the injured portion of the house fell
with a crash.

We fled, panic-stricken, into the street. If
it were the guns of an advancing enemy, better to meet them than to be buried in the ruins
of the house. My old servants clung about
me, shivering and shaking with terror.

"Don't wait to git nuffin' mo' on, Miss Rachel," exclaimed Uncle Ned—for I was bare-
headed, and clothed only in the lightest of
summer garments. "I know de day o' jedg-
ment's come, an' you ain't gwine to hab no use

fer bunnits an' sech truck in glory. Come 'long, honey, come 'long."

"But if the judgment has come, we may as well remain here," I said.

The most lurid description I could write would convey but a slight idea of the remaining hours of that night, and how they were passed by the people of Atlanta. At first we were firmly convinced that the Federal guns were turned against the wretched city, and that scarcely a stick or stone of it would be left by morning. People who had been asleep ran out of their houses and along the streets, huddling on such garments as they were able to pick up in their flight.

"The Yankees are coming!"

"Which way?"

"Are they fighting again?"

"Lord! Lord! when and where will it all end?"

Such were some of the exclamations and inquiries I heard.

"They must be blowing up the foundations

of the universe!" said one citizen, passing us barefooted, and with an old gown wrapped about his person.

The fears of the people were somewhat calmed when it was learned that the Confederates were destroying car-loads of ammunition and blowing up engine boilers, and that it was not the guns of an invading enemy. But the awful uproar—and I cannot find language strong enough and vivid enough to describe it—kept thousands of people on the streets until morning. Many houses had been so injured during the siege that it was dangerous to venture into them while such shocks were coming every moment, and shaking the very earth beneath our feet.

I could not help thinking of the destruction of Pompeii, and if streams of red-hot lava had flowed through the streets of Atlanta that night I should not have been in the least surprised. We went out on a hill, not far away from the house—an isolated pine grove left in the midst of the city, and spent the remainder of the night there. Uncle Ned and Aunt Milly passed the time alternately praying, weeping, or entreating me to prepare myself to go to glory.

"Dis yeth ain't gwine ter stan' much mo' sech ca'yin' on. Don't yer feel it shakin', honey? It's gwine to bust all ter flinders putty soon," said Uncle Ned.

"An' ef it does, whar'll we be?" sobbed Aunt Milly.

"None but er foolish 'oman 'ud ax dat question," replied her husband, with a contempt her temper would not submit to.

"Well, it'll send you a-flyin' down'ards, ef you don't look out!" she exclaimed.

"Ef it does I mighty feered you'll be a-kitin' 'longside o' me."

"Huh! I'll not be 'sociatin' wid no sech nigger as you when I gits to glory!"

As a quarrel seemed imminent, I hurriedly ordered them to be silent, and they fell to praying again as fervently as ever.

The work of destruction ended about dawn, and the citizens crept back to their shattered

houses, groping through clouds of thick, sul-
phurous smoke, spent with the night's watching.
But new anxieties and dangers had to be met.
All protection had been withdrawn from us—
all law and order. Robbery and deeds of violence of all kinds could be perpetrated, if men
were so minded, but beyond plundering stores
and dwellings deserted by their owners, the
mobs collecting on the streets were rather quiet.
I will not describe the hours of suspense the
defenseless Atlantians had to live through before the invading army took possession of the
city. I looked forward to the coming of the
Federals with mingled joy and dread. The
possibility of seeing Arnold again before the
close of the day compensated me for everything.
I could not sleep, though I felt the necessity of
refreshing myself with some rest after the exciting, wakeful night. I had not given much
thought to my personal appearance for a long
time. Graver, more important matters than
the preservation of my beauty had occupied my
mind, but when, about noon that day, Aunt

Milly burst into my room to tell me that Union soldiers were marching through the streets, I sprang up, and the first thing I did was to run to the glass, and look at myself. My face was pale and haggard; dark lines were drawn under my eyes. I turned dissatisfiedly away, but, in watching the Federal troops marching by, I soon forgot myself again.

I stared at every blue-coated officer from behind the jalousies, with anxious, eager eyes, searching for my beloved, but he did not appear. All the afternoon I watched and waited; then I said he would come at night, but it also passed without bringing him. Thus two days went by. The morning of the third, the following notice was served on the citizens:

'HEADQUARTERS POST OF ATLANTA, }
    "ATLANTA, GA., Sept. 5, 1864.   }

"GENERAL ORDERS, }
    "NO. 3.   }

"All families now living in Atlanta, the male representatives of which are in the service of the Confederate States, or who have gone South, will leave the city within five days. They will be passed through the lines, and will go South.

"All citizens from the North, not connected with the army, and who have not authority from Major-General Sherman or Major-General Thomas to remain in the city, will leave within the time above mentioned. If found within the city after that date they will be imprisoned.

"All male residents of this city, who do not register their names with the city Provost-Marshal within five days and receive authority to remain here, will be imprisoned.

"WM. COGSWELL,
"Colonel Commanding Post."

Our conquerors had been far more lenient than we had expected, but Judge Lenoir read this notice, and ordered us to pack our trunks and be ready to leave by noon.

"To-morrow—can we not wait until to-morrow?" I pleaded. "The notice gives five days."

He looked at me, a certain pity blending with the stern disapproval in his eyes.

"Further waiting will do no good, if it is your wretched husband you wish to see. I should have left the day the Yankees came in, had I not desired to give him an opportu-

nity to claim you. He has had ample time,
Rachel."

"Perhaps he was wounded at Jonesboro', or
his duties have detained him," I said, in a choking tone.

"He might have sent you some message.
False to his country, false to his wife."

"I will not believe that, sir. You are unjust,
cruel. He would come; I know he would come,
if he could."

"If you wish to remain in Atlanta alone and
unprotected, and surrounded by hordes of lawless soldiers, I will not prevent you, but I must
tell you that it will be a perilous thing to do."

I have since wished that I had been brave
enough to do it, but, inexperienced and fearful,
I could not make up my mind to take such a step.
I felt more like a captive being dragged away
to imprisonment than a refugee fleeing from an
enemy, while Aunt Milly and Uncle Ned hastily
gathered my personal property together. We
were to go in private conveyances as far as
Decatur, then by rail to Augusta. Mrs. Sims

was sorely grieved to leave all her precious household goods, but the judge impatiently ordered her to let them alone. At the last moment I begged Elinor to give me Arnold's picture, and she did so. It was a strange, hurried departure. We saw none of our friends, not even the Mandevilles, who were boarding in another part of the city. The house was closed and locked. I felt a dreadful sinking of the heart, as I followed the others out to the gate. It seemed to me that I ought to stay in Atlanta; that I ought to make inquiries about Arnold.

We were in the carriage when a Union soldier came up, saluted us, and said:

" Is this Judge Lenoir's family ? "

" It is," said the judge, haughtily, slamming the door in his face. I pulled down the window.

" What do you want ? " I cried, eagerly.

" To give this to Mrs. Arnold Lambert," drawing a sealed envelope from his pocket. " Captain Andrews asked me to deliver it. He was called away two days ago."

"Drive on!" said the judge angrily to the coachman.

"I am Mrs. Arnold Lambert!" I cried, as the horses started.

The soldier ran nearer, tossed the letter into my lap, but before he could utter another word of explanation we had rolled away.

"It is beneath you, Rachel, to parley with a common soldier, and a Yankee," said the judge.

I made no reply. With shaking fingers I tore open the envelope, my heart beating with the joyful anticipation of a letter from Arnold, a letter explaining his absence and silence; but my eyes seemed smitten with blindness as they fell on a ribbon-badge, marked with the Union colors, and with "Jonesboro', August 31st," traced in one corner, by an unfamiliar hand. Judge Lenoir sat opposite me. I held out the crumpled strip of silk to him.

"You will forgive him, now that he is dead," I said, then fell back, losing consciousness for the first time in my life.

CHAPTER XXIV.

IT was a long time before I came back to
clear rational thought. I took strange jour-
neys into still stranger countries. I traveled
through dry and thirsty desert lands, over
mountains so steep and rugged that my feet
could scarcely climb them, and into cities where
hostile faces constantly surrounded me, always
seeking Arnold, but never finding him. My
fevered brain held only one idea—to find him,
to vindicate his truth and honor. My surroundings, the people who came and went about me,
were matters I felt utterly indifferent to.

I had never been stricken with such illness
before, and the fever, which had doubtless been
coming on for some time, was aggravated by
the terrors and anxieties of the siege and the
final shock of receiving proof of Arnold's death.
I came back into the every-day world very
slowly. I first observed that I lay in my own

room at home, that Alicia, Nell, and even
Uncle Charles came and went constantly about
the bed. I felt too weak and tired to speak to
them, to even lift my hand or utter a word of
thanks when nourishments were offered to me.
I didn't feel particularly grateful for such ministrations. I would have much preferred being
left entirely alone. Aunt Milly hung constantly
about the bed and Uncle Ned kept the fire
blazing with fresh logs.

" How is her gittin' on now ? " he would whisper, asking the question every time he came in.

Elinor and her mother also sat in the room
occasionally, and one day I was startled to
hear the judge's voice at the door. No one but
Mrs. Sims was in the room, and she went to the
door.

" Come in, father."

" Is she asleep, Lizette ? " he inquired.

" I don't know. She is in the same state that
she was in yesterday. It is a most unnatural
condition, and *I* think that she will come out of
it only to die."

" Hush ! " he said, as he stepped softly across
the threshold.

" Oh, she cannot hear. She takes no notice
of anything."

Through half-closed eyelids I saw him as he
crossed the room and stood at the bedside,
looking very old and feeble, and leaning on his
stick. The soft expression of his face reminded
me of the first time that I had seen him and
compared him to Goethe. The recollection
touched such chords of memory that my whole
being seemed to vibrate. I sighed shud.dering-
ly. The wave of feeling seemed to leave me
colder and more indifferent than ever. I opened
my eyes and stared at him. It must have been
a very blank gaze, for he laid his tremulous old
hand on my head and said:

" Don't you know me, Rachel ? "

He was the last person I had spoken to before the beginning of my illness, and the first
as I came out of it. It was with a sense of
wonder at my own strength that I said:

" Yes, sir, I know you."

"God be thanked for that!" he cried fervently.

"I gave you the badge," I continued.

"Yes," and his face grew more and more agitated. "It is here," touching his breast pocket.

"May—I—have—it?"

"There, there, child, don't talk any more. Had I better call the others, father?" exclaimed Mrs. Sims in a frightened tone.

I knew she thought that I was dying, but life and death were alike indifferent to me. The judge drew the Union colors from his pocket and placed them in my hand. The sight of the cause of all my woe roused no special emotion in me, beyond a mournful satisfaction that I once more held the bit of ribbon Arnold had worn about his person.

My recovery was slow. The woods were changing their brilliant autumn tints to brown when I sat up by the window and looked into the outer world for the first time, a wan, ghostly shadow of myself. Illness had brought a cer-

tain patient resignation to me. I meditated on
my broken life with a calmness really astonish-
ing in one of such strong, ardent feelings as
mine. No tears, nor violent outbursts of grief,
nor vainly uttered regrets. I talked very little
at all, and those about me were wise enough to
leave me in peaceful silence. Judge Lenoir
came in to sit awhile with me every day. He
was very tender, remorsefully tender. Once he
reverted to the day we left Atlanta.

"I was brutally cruel," he said. "Rachel,
my child, you must forgive me."

"Oh, you didn't know; I couldn't blame
you," I replied, surprised that he should let such
a little thing trouble him.

"But I might have been kinder."

"It doesn't matter now," I said gently.

"Does anything matter now, Rachel?"

"Not to me."

Later Elinor told me that Arnold's death had
affected the judge very much; that all his love
for the boy, as he called him, had risen warm
and tender in his heart again; that secretly he

grieved deeply. I felt glad of it, and the old man seemed nearer and dearer to me afterward.

As I took up the threads of daily life again, certain changes became evident. One day I looked out on the "quarters," and saw that most of the cabins were vacant. Here and there a feeble old man or woman appeared, but the children, the strong, lusty young negroes, and the middle-aged, were all gone.

" Where are all the negroes ? " I inquired.

" Gone to the Yankees," said Nell, in a tone of extreme disgust. " Father says that they will be glad enough to get back again, but he is not sure that he will allow one of them on the place. I wouldn't, I'm sure. Ungrateful creatures, to run away from their best friends ! Would you believe it, Rachel, I actually have to dress myself ! We've scarcely servants enough left to do the housework."

" How did I get home ? " was the next question I asked.

" They brought you in the carriage. It was an awful shock to us when they drove up with

20

you, white as a ghost, and—and limp as a rag.
We thought at first that you were dead, and
when we heard that you were married, and
what had happened—well, if war didn't give
one nerves of iron, there'd be no living through
it.   We were already quite distracted about
you, shut up in Atlanta.   I really never passed
through such a harassing year in all my life."

She did seem greatly changed and sobered.
Her dress was plain and simple, and the beautiful coquettish curls were all pinned back.

From her I learned that Arnold's people
were in their own house, that they gave up all
thought of going to Augusta, but settled down
at the Montgomery place to be near me during
my illness.

" They stopped here for a few days until the
house could be opened, or put in order, rather,
for it was broken open months ago, and half
the things in it destroyed."

There were other questions I wished to ask,
but she was called away to attend to some
household duty. Some change in Alicia vague-

ly troubled me. The sweet and tender melancholy of her face touched me with a sense of pain every time I looked at her, and why, I wondered, should she wear a black gown all the time ? I remembered it as one that I particularly disliked.

"I wish you wouldn't wear this," I said to her once, touching its folds with the tips of my fingers.

"It is all the black gown I have," she replied, with a slight quiver in her voice.

"Why must you wear black?" I asked in a whisper.

"You have not heard ?"

"I have not heard anything."

"Reuben was killed in the battle of Atlanta."

I could not utter one word of sympathy. I simply looked up at her and held out my hand. She came nearer; threw her arm about my neck.

"I felt for you as the others could not," she whispered, "for I knew by experience what you suffered."

I felt her tears falling on my face, and leaned against her, my own eyes wet with the first bitter drops I had shed since Arnold's death.

We talked together for a long time, and it seemed to me that I had just begun to realize what a strong, brave woman my cousin was.

"Now," she said at last, rising, "can you walk into my room? I want to show you something."

She wrapped a mantle around me, and I followed her down the hall to her bedroom. A crib stood near the hearth, and leading me up to it, she turned back the blankets from a rosy sleeping baby. I caught my breath in a little gasp.

"Yours, Alicia?" looking across at her face in a tremulous glow of love and tenderness.

"Yes, mine," she said, with such deep joy in the ownership, I felt glad for her. "My son, my Reuben!"

"When—when——"

"He was born just two weeks before—his father fell in that battle."

" Did *he* know ? "

" My husband ? Yes; I had written a few lines, and he wrote to me the day before he died."

The child opened his eyes, and seeing a strange face bending over him, cried out with terror.

Alicia lifted him in her arms to her breast, pressing his round tender face against her heart.

" You are not alone," I said.

" No, I shall never be alone while he lives," and she looked at me with soft, pitying eyes.

A light tap on the door interrupted us. "Come," said Alicia, and a big loose-jointed negro man came shyly in, twisting his wool hat around in his hands. It was John, Cousin Reuben's personal attendant.

" Didn't I hear Mars Rubin cryin', Missus ? "

" Yes, you may take him down-stairs, John."

He took the child into his big arms, holding it tenderly as a woman, and it nestled contentedly on his shoulder, its fair, sweet face lying

against his black neck.   When he went out of
the room Alicia told me of his grief for the loss
of his master, and his devotion to the baby.
He would hold the child by the hour, and could
pacify and amuse it when no one else could.
As we talked we went to the window and
looked out into the back yard.   There sat John
on the kitchen doorstep, in the sunshine, with
little Reuben on his knee, crooning a lullaby
in his husky voice.

Mutual sympathy drew Alicia and me very
close together during those days of my conval-
escence.   Uncle Charles was too bewildered by
the general state of affairs to do much more
than wander about the house and plantation,
helplessly wondering how he could get on
without his slaves.   The sight of the deserted
" quarters " seemed to smite him with sad surprise every day.

" Who would have thought it ? " he said, one
day, standing on the back piazza, with his
hands in his pockets, staring down at the vacant cabins.

"Thought what, Uncle Charles?"

"That the war would turn out as it has, and that the ungrateful negroes I've fed and clothed so long would run away and leave me, the first chance they could get."

I knew that it would be useless for me to argue that the negroes earned their food and clothing: his sense of injury would remain; so I held my peace. It was Alicia who told me how they had suffered from the ravages of the army. All the horses and cattle, almost every fowl, had been taken away from the place, and the house would have been pillaged one day by a party of the common soldiers—"bummers," they were called—had not an officer interfered. Fences were torn down, carts and wagons destroyed, and one day she went with me to the carriage-house, to show the sad plight of the handsome new carriage Uncle Charles had bought soon after our return to Georgia. Its cushions were torn open; its purple silk lining hung in tatters.

"They cut it to pieces with their pocket-

knives," she said. " I asked them why they
wantonly destroyed our unoffending property,
and they said that it was the only way to conquer us."

While we were on that tour of inspection,
she carried me down into the orchard, where
the turf grew thick and green under an apple-
tree. She stooped down near a gnarled root
and spread open the grass.

" It doesn't show where it has been cut,
does it ? "

" Cut ! " I echoed; " how ? "

She rose up, brushing her fingers.

" When we heard that the Yankees were
coming, father felt distracted about his money.
He didn't know what to do with it. I told him
that I would hide it. I put it in an iron pot—
one that had a cover to it—came down here
one night, after twelve o'clock, and buried it.
I cut out a square of the sod, and lifted it up
whole. When I had buried the pot, I replaced
the grass as you see it now. No one knew
where it was—not even father nor Nell. I used

to tremble when the soldiers were prowling
through the orchard. They walked over this
very spot dozens of times, and once I slipped
down here and thrust a stick into the ground,
to make sure the pot had not been removed.
Ought we to leave it here?"

" By all means, until the country is in a safer,
more settled state," I replied.

"The Federal troops still occupy Atlanta."

" Yes, and they forage all through the country."

It was that night that Nell ran into my room,
crying:

" Wake up, Rachel! wake up! They are
burning Atlanta!"

I sprang up, my weakened nerves thrilling
with the shock of such news. All the front
windows of the house were illuminated with a
strong, red light, and, in the rear, the orchard,
the negro quarters, and the woods and fields
beyond, were like a vivid picture against a background of darkness. Uncle Charles and the
girls, and two or three of the negroes, climbed

out on the roof, but I was forbidden to expose myself in the night air, on account of my recent illness. I stood by the front window, with Uncle Ned and Aunt Milly hovering near me. My heart swelled with pain; tears streamed silently down my cheeks. In Atlanta I had experienced my greatest joy and bitterest sorrow, and its destruction seemed to break the last link between me and that past. But my tears quenched not one spark of the fire. Up the clouded sky streamed the lurid light until all the world seemed one vast conflagration.

CHAPTER XXV.

IT was midsummer, and nearly two months after the surrender. The turmoil of war had ceased, though many people could yet scarcely believe no more battles would be fought. The country was still in an agitated condition, and bade fair to remain so for a long time; but it was the natural result of such a fierce struggle, such a great revolution. It affected all classes, none more than the planters, who had to learn to adjust themselves to narrowed circumstances and to hired labor in place of their slaves. Many of them were ruined, through lack of knowledge and experience to manage their affairs under the changed conditions.

Some of Uncle Charles's negroes strayed back to him after the first excitement and intoxication of freedom had worn off, and they realized that they would still have to work for a living.

He was not inclined to take them back as wage-
earners, but Alicia wisely counseled that they
would be better than strangers on the place,
and he listened to her. Poor Uncle Charles,!
Had it not been for her his experiments as a
planter after the war would have ended in dis-
astrous failure. She curtailed all lavish expen-
diture, and gradually led him to see the necessity for planting less land than when he had
an army of slaves at his beck and call.

Wifehood and motherhood had developed
and strengthened latent qualities in my cousin
unsuspected in her girlhood. She led a busy,
absorbed life, devoted to the care of the household, her father's interests, and the love of her
child. She seemed to find more and more
pleasure in living for him, in watching his
growth, planning his future, as the winter passed and spring brought peace to the country.
She grew cheerful, and talked less, even to me,
of her sorrow and loss; but in the twilight,
when the baby was tucked into his crib, asleep,
she would steal away and walk alone through

the grounds, and, by the gentle sadness of her
face, I knew that it was an hour devoted to
Cousin Reuben.

After the surrender I told Uncle Ned and
Aunt Milly that they were free, and could
leave me, if they desired to do so.

" Now, Miss Rachel, what is I done dat you
gwine ter talk so?" exclaimed the old man, in
a tone of mingled grief and indignation. " Don't
I al'ays min' you? 'ceptin' I did foller you ter
Chattanugy dat time. Co'se, if you wants ter
git rid o' me an' Milly, you can sell us; but I
know ole mars 'lowed——"

" I cannot do anything of the kind. I have
no power to buy or sell you. You are a citizen
of the United States, and as free as I am."

" Law, honey, me an' Ned done b'long ter
you too many years now for changes," said
Aunt Milly.

" Of course, I don't want you to leave me,
but I do want you to understand that you
have the liberty to do it, if you desire to. If
you remain I will pay you wages."

They treated that proposition as a kind of joke. I had always shown a certain liberality toward them, and they had some money laid by. They would have served me faithfully the remainder of their lives without a penny more, and when, at the end of the first month of their freedom, I paid them wages, they received it gratefully, as a gift; and it was so as long as they lived. They counted their services as something rightfully mine, and not to be paid for.

I received a letter from Miss Jane Mandeville soon after the surrender. They had returned to their plantation, near Cartersville, and were extremely poor. I pondered a good deal over a long letter received from Mary Ladislaw late in the spring.

"I have decided, dear Rachel, to undertake a rather strange work," she wrote. "To lead an idle life will be impossible for me after the busy, stirring years we have just passed through, and after my grievous loss. My relatives are most kind, and desire me to remain with them,

but I must have employment for my heart and
brain, to keep me from brooding, to keep me
from melancholy — madness.   I have still a
small portion of property, and I intend to open
an industrial school for the instruction of poor
children, left orphans by the war. Those of the
better classes will be cared for, but I wish to
give useful training to the humble, ignorant
girls left helpless and unprovided for. They
should be a sacred trust to the South, these
orphans of the Confederacy.   Our slaves are
now free citizens, and it yet remains to be seen
whether, under such circumstances, they will
make good servants.

"I shall not remain in Savannah to make
this experiment, my relatives are all so prej-
udiced against it. They call it a wild scheme,
an occupation lowering to my dignity. I verily
believe they would rather see me a sister of
charity, but the spirit of a missionary animates
me. If to teach poor children requires the giving up of social position, I am willing to make
the sacrifice, and to spend all the remaining

years of my life in this work. I think not only
of the benefit to the individual, but of the
ultimate good of the country. Dense ignorance prevails among our lower classes."

This letter surprised, almost shocked me at
first, and I hastily implored Mary to carefully
consider all that such an undertaking would
involve, but the more I thought it over, the
more noble and righteous it seemed. I will
state here that her plan was never a thorough
success, and she finally gave it up, after her
money had all been expended, and accepted a
position as teacher in a college, to the chagrin
of her relatives, who could never overcome
the traditional prejudice against women working.

That spring of the surrender I was strangely
tempted to join her, my life seemed so idle and
purposeless. That the world could ever hold
any great interest for me again seemed impossible. My brief and tragical love-story had
closed the doors of happiness against me forever. Arnold Lambert had absorbed my heart

too entirely for me to ever think of loving another. I said very little about him, but his image remained as vividly impressed on my heart as it had ever been. There had been a sorrowful pilgrimage to the Jonesboro' battle-field with Judge Lenoir and Elinor, but we could find no trace of him. He had evidently been buried with the unknown dead. What to do with the future I knew not. Alicia had her duties and would in time grow happy and contented in them, and Nell expected soon to be married. I stitched many sad reflections into her *trousseau*.

Judge Lenoir had repeatedly urged me to make my home with his family. They had gone back to Atlanta, and as their house had escaped the general destruction repaired it at considerable cost. I visited it once, but every room seemed so haunted with memories of Arnold, that I shrank from living in them altogether.

It was Nell's wedding eve, and when the last stitches had been taken in the bridal dress

21

I left the house and went down to the Montgomery place to inspect the roses in the
garden. They were destined to adorn the wedding feast, and the parlor next day. It was
the softest and stillest of June evenings. The
twilight came down lingeringly, indeed there
was scarcely any twilight at all, for in the west
the rose of sunset shone, while in the east the
full moon came up.

It had been one of my dark, rebellious days.
I did not grudge Nell her happiness, but it
seemed most bitter that mine should be taken
from me.

" If you can see me, and know my wretched-
ness, comfort me with your presence, my beloved!" I cried, my streaming eyes lifted to the
empty vault of the sky. I paced the garden
walks until only the moonlight made a soft
illumination about me, and stars sparkled in
the blue of the upper heaven. Then I turned
toward the gate again. As I did so a man
thrust it open with a quick, imperious gesture,
and approached me. I stopped for a moment,

wondering who it could be, then I stood still because surprise, joy—I know not what indescribable emotion—held me speechless and motionless, for it was Arnold walking toward me with those impatient steps, those love-lit eyes, and outstretched arms. Could it be a vision, a mere phantasm conjured up by my own eyes, yearning to behold him? Were not those arms, gathering me into an impassioned embrace, real? those lips touching mine, warm and tender with life?

The light of a new existence seemed to dawn upon me when I at last realized that my husband had not perished on the battle-field, but stood at my side, living, and bidding me to come forth with him into a world made glorious by his love and companionship.

THE END.

Mark Twain's Books.

Adventures of Huckleberry Finn.
Holiday edition. Square 8vo, 366 pages. Illustrated by E. W. Kemble. Sheep, $3.25;
cloth, ... $2 75

New Cheap Edition of Huckleberry Finn.
12mo, 318 pages, with a few illustrations.
Cloth, ... $1 00

The Prince and the Pauper.
A square 8vo volume of 411 pages. Beautifully
illustrated. Sheep $3.75; cloth, $3 00

A Connecticut Yankee in King Arthur's Court.
A square 8vo of 575 pages; 221 illustrations by
Dan Beard. Half morocco, $5.00; sheep,
$4.00; cloth, . $3 00

Mark Twain Holiday Set.

Three volumes in a box, consisting of the best editions of "Huckleberry Finn," "Prince and Pauper," and "A Connecticut Yankee." Square 8vo. Uniform in size, binding, and color. Sold only in sets. Cloth, . . $6 00

Eighteen Short Stories and Sketches.

By Mark Twain. Including, "The Stolen White Elephant," "Some Rambling Notes," "The Carnival of Crime," "A Curious Experience," "Punch, Brothers, Punch," "The Invalid's Story," etc., etc. 16mo, 306 pages. Cloth, ... $1 00

Mark Twain's "Library of Humor."

A volume of 145 Characteristic Selections from the Best Writers, together with a Short Biographical Sketch of Each Author Quoted. Compiled by Mark Twain. Nearly 200 illustrations by E. W. Kemble. 8vo, 707 pages. Full Turkey morocco, $7.00; half morocco, $5.00; half seal, $4.25; sheep, $4.00; cloth, $3 50

Life on the Mississippi.

8vo, 624 pages; and over 300 illustrations. Sheep, $4.25; cloth, . . . $3 50

We also furnish Mark Twain's earlier writings, as follows:

Innocents Abroad;
   or, The New Pilgrim's Progress.   Sheep, $4.00;
   cloth, ... $3 50

Roughing It.
   600 pages; 300 illustrations.   Sheep, $4.00;
   cloth, ... $3 50

Sketches, Old and New.
   320 pages; 122 illustrations.   Sheep, $3.50;
   cloth, ... $3 00

Adventures of Tom Sawyer.
   150 engravings; 275 pages.   Sheep, $3.25;
   cloth, ... $2 75

The Gilded Age.
   576 pages; 212 illustrations.   Sheep, $4.00;
   cloth, ... $3 50

A Tramp Abroad. Mark Twain in Europe.
   A Companion Volume to " Innocents Abroad."
   631 pages.   Sheep, $4.00; cloth, $3 50

The War Series.

The Genesis of the Civil War.
The Story of Sumter, by Major-General S. W. Crawford, A. M., M. D., LL. D. Illustrated with steel and wood engravings and fac-similes of celebrated letters. 8vo, uniform with Grant's Memoirs. Full morocco, $8.00; half morocco, $5.50; sheep, $4.25; cloth,   .   . $3 50

Personal Memoirs of General Grant.
Illustrations and maps, etc. 2 vols.; 8vo. Half morocco, per set, $11.00; sheep, per set, $9.00; cloth, per set, $7.00. A few sets in full Turkey morocco and tree calf for sale at special low prices.

Personal Memoirs of General Sherman.
With appendix by Hon. James G. Blaine. Illustrated; 2 vols.; 8vo, uniform with Grant's Memoirs. Half morocco, per set, $8.50; sheep, per set, $7.00; cloth, per set,   .   . $5 00
Cheap edition, in one large volume. Cloth, $2 00

Personal Memoirs of General Sheridan.
Illustrated with steel portraits and woodcuts; 26 maps; 2 vols.; 8vo, uniform with Grant's Memoirs. Half morocco, per set, $10.00; sheep, per set, $8.00; cloth, per set, $6.00. A few sets in full Turkey morocco and tree calf to be disposed of at very low figures. Cheap edition, in one large volume, cloth binding, $2 00

McClellan's Own Story.

With illustrations from sketches drawn on the field of battle by A. R. Waud, the Great War Artist. 8vo, uniform with Grant's Memoirs. Full morocco, $9.00; half morocco, $6.00; sheep, $4.75; cloth, . . . $3 75

Reminiscences of Winfield Scott Hancock.

By his wife. Illustrated; steel portraits of General and Mrs. Hancock; 8vo, uniform with Grant's Memoirs. Full morocco, $5.00; half morocco, $4.00; sheep, $3.50; cloth, $2 75

Tenting on the Plains.

With the Life of General Custer, by Mrs. E. B. Custer. Illustrated; 8vo, uniform with Grant's Memoirs. Full morocco, $7.00; half morocco, $5.50; sheep, $4.25; cloth, . $3 50

The Great War Library.

Consisting of the best editions of the foregoing seven publications (Grant, Sheridan, Sherman, Hancock, McClellan, Custer and Crawford). Ten volumes in a box; uniform in style and binding. Half morocco, $50.00; sheep, $40.00; cloth, ... $30 00

Portrait of General Sherman.

A magnificent line etching on copper; size, 19x24 inches; by the celebrated artist, Charles B. Hall. $2.00. (Special prices on quantities.)

Other Biographical Works.

Life of Jane Welsh Carlyle.
By Mrs. Alexander Ireland. With portrait and fac-simile letter; 8vo, 324 pages. Vellum cloth, gilt top, ... $1 75

Life and Letters of Roscoe Conkling.
By Hon. Alfred R. Conkling, Ph. B., LL. D.; steel portrait and fac-similes of important letters to Conkling from Grant, Arthur, Garfield, etc. 8vo, over 700 pages. Half morocco, $5.50; full seal, $5.00; sheep, $4.00; cloth, $3 00

Biography of Ephraim McDowell, M. D.
The Father of Abdominal Surgery, by his granddaughter, Mrs. Mary Young Ridenbaugh; also McDowell's Operations of Ovariotomy, by Nathan Bozeman, M. D.; bound together in an octavo volume. 558 pages; illustrated. Bound in half morocco, . . . $5 50

Life of Pope Leo XIII.
By Bernard O'Reilly, D. D., L. D. (Laval.) Written with the encouragement and blessing of His Holiness, the Pope. 8vo, 635 pages; colored and steel plates, and full-page illustrations. Half morocco, $6.00; half Russia, $5.00; cloth, gilt edges, ... $3 75

Miscellaneous.

The Table.

How to Buy Food, How to Cook It, and How to Serve It, by A. Filippini, of Delmonico's; the only cook-book ever endorsed by Delmonico; contains three menus for each day in the year, and over 1,500 original recipes, the most of which have been guarded as secrets by the *chefs* of Delmonico. Contains the simplest as well as the most elaborate recipes. Presentation edition in full seal Russia, $4.50; Kitchen edition in oil-cloth, ... $2 50

Yale Lectures on Preaching,

and other Writings, by Rev. Nathaniel Burton, D. D.; edited by Richard E. Burton. 8vo. 640 pages; steel portrait. Cloth, $3 75

Concise Cyclopedia of Religious Knowledge.

Biblical, Biographical, Theological, Historical, and Practical; edited by Rev. E. B. Sanford, M. A., assisted by over 30 of the most eminent religious scholars in the country. 1 vol.; royal 8vo, nearly 1,000 double-column pages. Half morocco, $6.00; sheep, $5.00; cloth, $3 50

Legends and Myths of Hawaii.

By the late King Kalakaua; two steel portraits and 25 other illustrations. 8vo, 530 pages. Cloth, ... $3 00

The Diversions of a Diplomat in Turkey.

By the late Hon. S. S. Cox. 8vo, 685 pages; profusely illustrated. Half morocco, $6.00; sheep, $4.75; cloth, ... $3 75

Inside the White House in War Times.

By W. O. Stoddard, one of Lincoln's Private Secretaries. 12mo, 244 pages. Cloth, $1 00

Tinkletop's Crime

and Eighteen other Short Stories, by George R. Sims. 1 vol.; 12mo, 316 pages. Cloth, $1.00; paper covers, . . 50 cents.

My Life with Stanley's Rear Guard.

By Herbert Ward, one of the Captains of Stanley's Rear Guard; includes Mr. Ward's Reply to H. M. Stanley. 12mo. Cloth, $1.00; paper covers, ... 50 cents.

The Peril of Oliver Sargent.

By Edgar Janes Bliss. 12mo. Cloth, $1.00; paper covers, ... 50 cents.

The Old Devil and the Three Little Devils;

or, Ivan The Fool, by Count Leo Tolstoi, translated direct from the Russian by Count Norraikow, with illustrations by the celebrated Russian artist, Gribayedoff. 12mo. Cloth, $1 00

Charles L. Webster & Co.

The Happy Isles,
    and Other Poems, by S. H. M. Byers. Small
    12mo. Cloth binding,   .   . $1 00

Physical Beauty:
    How to Obtain and How to Preserve It, by
    Annie Jenness Miller; including chapters on
    Hygiene, Foods, Sleep, Bodily Expression, the
    Skin, the Eyes, the Teeth, the Hair, Dress, the
    Cultivation of Individuality, etc., etc. An
    octavo volume of about 300 pages. Cloth, $2 00

For sale by all booksellers, or sent, by mail or express prepaid, by the publishers,

CHARLES L. WEBSTER & CO.,
67 Fifth Avenue, New York City.

www.ingramcontent.com/pod-product-compliance
Lightning Source LLC
Chambersburg PA
CBHW020944030726
47496CB00005B/1341